This Book ~

~~[illegible]~~

Terre Haute, Indiana

W-145? November 26, 1957

THE GABRIEL HORN

Young People's Edition

THE
GABRIEL HORN

YOUNG PEOPLE'S EDITION

BY

FELIX HOLT

EST. 1852

E. P. DUTTON & CO., INC.

NEW YORK, 1953

Library of Congress Catalog Card Number: 52-12948

TO

MARGIE AND PAT

CHAPTER I

THE Cumberlands were a month behind us when we came to
the Cadiz toll road. A night and another day would bring our
journey to The Purchase to an end, so Big Eli and I were stepping an easy pace. Our hunting dog, Faro, was taking his time
too and now and then he would lie down in the dusty road to
wait for us to catch up with him. We had traveled the toll road
a mile or so when he bristled and growled. Ahead of us was a
stagecoach with the left rear wheel sagged to the ground like a
wounded rabbit dragging a leg. The broken wheel was on the
ground beside it and three men were looking on. Two of them
were wearing dusters and they were arguing with the driver,
a skinny little man in shiny boots and green coat, but they
stopped to watch us as we came up.

The driver asked Big Eli, "Are you going to Cadiz, my
good man?"

"Through it," said Big Eli.

"Then stop at the blacksmith's and have him fetch us a
wheel," said the driver.

Big Eli reached down with his right hand and took hold of
the sagging axle. Then, as easy as picking up his hat, he raised
it to hip level. "Why don't you histe it like this and run along-
side to Cadiz?" he said in fun.

The two men in dusters laughed but the little driver didn't.
Big Eli let the axle back to the ground and wiped his hands on
his buckskin britches. "I'll see the smithy," he said like he was
sorry for poking fun at the driver.

The driver looked at the Gabriel Horn swinging from the
rawhide thong over Big Eli's shoulder. "You're a hunter?" he
asked and Big Eli said he was. The driver reached up to the
high seat of the coach and brought down a long brass horn
that looked like a candle taper. He wiped the dust from it with
his coat sleeve.

7

"You can outlift me," he said, "but I'm betting I can outblow you."

"I've got no betting money," said Big Eli.

"Then I dast you for nothing," the little driver said.

Big Eli didn't say anything. He handed me the long rifle and eased his head and big shoulders through the rawhide thong of the Gabriel Horn. "What's the rules?" he asked.

"How many blows can you make with one breath?" the driver asked him.

"I never counted," said Big Eli. "How many can you make?"

"More than you," said the driver.

The two men in dusters grinned at each other.

Big Eli's chest began to swell. I was glad he had unlaced his jacket that afternoon when the sun got so hot. Laces and buttons wouldn't hold when Big Eli sucked wind to blow the Gabriel Horn.

"Go!" said the driver, and began counting as the first blast came out of the Gabriel Horn as cool and clear as dew on a spider web.

When the first echo came back from the ridge of hills to the west I was certain that the two men in dusters would agree that our hunting horn sounded prettier than the brass coach horn even if Big Eli should lose on blows. Big Eli had cut it off a swamp steer in Carolina the year I was born and it had taken him two years to season and scrape it paper thin. Nobody but Big Eli had ever blown it, though once I had asked him to let me try.

"It takes a man's wind to blow the Gabriel Horn," he said. "Someday you'll grow up to it, Little Eli."

Once I asked him why he called it the Gabriel Horn and he laughed. "Come Judgment Day, the Archangel Gabriel will want to swap," he said.

As I stood there on the Cadiz toll road listening to him blow I wondered if the Archangel Gabriel had a brass horn like the coach driver's.

"Seven . . . eight . . . nine," I heard the driver counting and then Big Eli lowered the Gabriel Horn, sucked in his breath and wiped his lips on his sleeve. The two men in dusters looked at the little coach driver.

"Your turn," said Big Eli.

The driver stepped back a pace and tossed his horn to the seat of the coach and when he faced Big Eli he was grinning.

"I couldn't tie that," he said. "You win."

I was mighty proud of Big Eli and our Gabriel Horn.

"Come on, Little Eli," he said to me and we started over the road toward Cadiz.

When we were out of earshot I said, "He bit off more than he could chaw."

"I'm not so certain," said Big Eli and I could tell by the way he said it that he thought the coach driver had made a fool of him in some way.

It was about an hour later, judging by the sun which was going down, when we got to Cadiz. It wasn't much of a place. Only a few houses and a tavern. People were standing in front of the tavern watching us as we came up the road. In front of the others was a fat man with an apron tied about his middle and beside him was a girl with red hair and freckles and she had on an apron too. I thought she was mighty pretty.

Big Eli spoke to Faro and he heeled as we came up to the crowd. "They'll tell us where to find the smithy," Big Eli said to me, but he never got a chance to ask. The fat man in the apron was looking at the Gabriel Horn swinging from Big Eli's shoulder.

"Did you blow that horn about an hour ago?" he asked Big Eli.

Big Eli nodded. "I did," he said.

"How many times did you blow it?" the fat man asked.

"Nine," said Big Eli. "Why?"

"You bought yourself nine chickens, mister," said the fat man, setting his lips as tight across his teeth as a closed bear trap. Everybody but the redheaded girl began to laugh at what the fat man said. She was looking at Big Eli's long yellow hair which tumbled over his broad shoulders.

"You're mistaken," said Big Eli.

The fat man's face was getting as red as a cock's comb.

"You'll pay for 'em!" he shouted and grabbed Big Eli by the sleeve of his buckskin jacket.

Big Eli shook him off. "Don't lay hold of me," he said.

The fat man started screaming and the others crowded around us. "I killed nine chickens when I heard that horn," the fat man yelled, "and you'll pay for 'em!"

I saw that Big Eli was getting mad. "Why did you kill them?" he asked.

"I thought it was the coach horn," said the fat man, "and you'll pay for 'em!"

"I'm light of money," Big Eli told him and he wasn't lying.

"Then you'll work it out," yelled fatty and he made another grab for Big Eli's arm.

Big Eli handed me the long rifle. "Hold the dog," he said.

As I got Faro by the scruff of the neck I saw Big Eli swing a flat hand. It smacked the fat man's jaw like the tail of a 'gator, reeling him into the crowd. "Now don't lay hold of me no more," said Big Eli.

"Arrest him, Constable!" the fat man screamed at a man about half the size of Big Eli. Big Eli grinned when he saw him.

"It'll take more than him," he said, laughing.

The Constable swept his eyes around the crowd. "I'll deputize the lot of y'," he said. "Let's take him!"

Big Eli clenched his fists and shifted his weight.

There was a rush and the girl screamed. Man after man went down as Big Eli swung his fists and kicked, but there were too many of them. They brought him down in the dust and sat on him until the Constable got out his wrist irons and locked them on Big Eli. I was holding to Faro and crying when they pulled Big Eli to his feet and began shoving him toward a stone smokehouse in back of the tavern.

"You come with me," I heard the redheaded girl say and I felt her soft hand on my shoulder. I looked up and saw that she was scared too, for there were tears in her eyes. The rifle had fallen in the dust and she picked it up. Faro and I followed her through the taproom into the kitchen of the tavern. As scared as I was, I smelled the odor of cooking chickens and remembered I hadn't anything to eat since Big Eli and I cooked a snack over a campfire at daybreak. She hurried to the open fireplace where two big skillets were resting on a bed of hot coals, and when she lifted the lids I counted nine chickens, all sputtering in their own grease. She saw me counting them and I saw her smile like she'd rather laugh but didn't dast.

"Old Decker thought it was the coach coming when he heard the horn," she said to me. "Nine blasts of the coach horn means nine passengers to feed."

Old Decker, I guessed, was the fat man in the apron.

Then I remembered the biggety little coach driver and I knew then why he didn't blow against Big Eli. He had got even with Big Eli for lifting the coach and making him look puny in front of two passengers.

The redheaded girl gave me a cup of milk and some cold biscuits. "That's enough for now," she said. I wished she hadn't brought me to the kitchen. After smelling the chickens in the skillets, milk and cold biscuits didn't taste so good, hungry as I was. I drank the milk and gave the biscuits to Faro.

It was long after dark when the two men in dusters came into the tavern and told what had happened on the toll road. I could see them in the taproom and hear them laughing when old Decker told them what had happened to Big Eli. They ate two of the chickens and old Decker and the Constable ate one apiece, leaving five still in the skillets. When they were through eating, the girl brought out the dishes and closed the door to the taproom.

"My name's Hannah," she said, and I told her mine was Little Eli Wakefield.

"Then his must be Big Eli," she said grinning, meaning Big Eli, and I said it was. She began slicing chicken and putting it on two plates. Then she dipped up slices of yellow yams that had been stewing in the chicken grease and over it all she ladled thick gravy. She put the plates on the table, one in front of me, and sat down. "Let's eat, Little Eli," she said.

I wondered if she was old Decker's kin, but she didn't look like him. It was my guess that she was about seventeen years old. Her dress seemed a little tight for her but it showed how round and firm she was. The light breeze that came through the open back door brought the faint scent of her to me and it pleasured me. When she smiled her eyes almost closed and her lips barely parted. She was the prettiest girl I had ever seen.

She asked me a lot of questions and I told her that Big Eli and I came from mountain country and that we were going to The Purchase, which was the new land west of the Tennessee that General Andy Jackson had bought from the Chickasaw Indians.

"Lots of folks are going there," she said, "but I hear that all of the good land has been bought up now."

"We're not going for land," I said. "I've got an uncle and aunt there."

"Visiting?" she asked.

"Big Eli got a letter from Uncle Zack," I said. "We'll live with him and Aunt Soph, I reckon."

"It's a wilderness, they tell," she said, "and the trees are so big they black the sky like night."

The door of the taproom opened and the fat man with the apron came in and looked at me and the plate full of vittles. Hannah saw him.

"He was hungry," she said.

Old Decker picked up my plate and she shouted, "Don't do that!" as he tossed the chicken and yams in the swill bucket. She started to get up from the chair but he slapped her across the face with the back of his hand. "Scraps are good enough for the likes of him," he said.

He pulled a bunch of keys from his belt and dropped them on the table. "I'm driving the smithy out the toll road to put a wheel on the coach," he said. "Lock up, come midnight."

He left by the back door and Hannah followed to the door where she stood listening until she heard him drive off.

She went to the cupboard and got out two plates and filled them with chicken, yams and gravy and gave one to me.

"Now finish your supper," she said, and then asked, "Does he hanker for grog or coffee with his vittles?"

I knew she meant Big Eli. "Coffee," I said, and she filled a

mug from a simmering pot on the coals. She took the mug and
the plate and disappeared through the back door, but she was
back in a few minutes and in the light of the turpentine lamp
swinging from the ceiling, I saw that her cheeks were pink
and there was a sparkle in her eyes which she tried to hide by
not looking at me. She began gathering up the dishes in the
taproom and bringing them into the kitchen. I finished my
plate while she fed scraps to Faro, then I curled up in a chair
by the open fireplace. She was washing dishes and singing as
soft as a whippoorwill when I dropped off to sleep.

I don't know when it was that I woke up with a start when
I felt a hand across my mouth. The lamp was out and the
only light came from the dull red coals in the fireplace. I was
scared stiff as a scarecrow, for I had forgot where I was.

"It's me," said Hannah in a whisper. "Don't be scared, but
don't make a sound." She took her hand from my face and I
rubbed my eyes with the back of my hand to clear them. I
could make out the wrist irons the Constable had locked on
Big Eli. They were on the table, and I saw a battered carpetbag on the hearth and Fargo was sniffing it. Big Eli's rifle was
stacked beside the carpetbag.

Hannah motioned at Faro. "Keep him quiet and come with
me," she said. She picked up the bag and the rifle while I got
hold of Faro's scruff, and we left by the back door.

There were stars but no moon, so I kept close to her but
soon I could make out the smokehouse where they had taken
Big Eli. When we got there he was outside waiting for us and
I knew then that she had let him out with old Decker's keys
while I slept. Faro started to whine when he saw Big Eli and
Big Eli had to speak sharp to shut him up. Faro seemed to
know something was afoot for he didn't go bounding off
through the woods, but stuck close at Big Eli's heels.

I yawned.

"He's too sleepy to walk," Hannah said.

"I'll tote him," said Big Eli, and with one arm he swung me
to his back. Then he took the carpetbag from Hannah.

"You tote the rifle," he said to her, and they started off.

I wasn't so sleepy that I wasn't wondering about Hannah

and why she was going with us and what she would do when we got to Uncle Zack's place in Humility. And though I was asking questions of myself that only time would answer, it pleasured me that she was going for it was the first time I had ever been so close to a woman and heard her sing and laugh and seen her cry. Somehow I felt I had known Hannah a long, long time.

As we passed the last house in the village, I heard a clock strike two.

CHAPTER II

THE sun was coming up when we saw the blue ribbon of the Cumberland winding through the bottom lands to the west of us. We hadn't been following a road or trail, but had kept to timber and I guessed that Big Eli didn't want anybody to see us.

"There's a place called Boyd's Tavern on the river," Hannah said. "We can cross there."

Big Eli shook his head. "We'd better stay clear of it," he said. "They'll be following us."

When we reached the river he began looking for dry driftwood to make a raft. There was plenty of it and he cut grapevines hanging from the trees and lashed the logs together. Then he cut a long pole and we shoved the raft into the stream. In the shake of a doe's tail we were crossing, with Big Eli doing the poling. When we got across, he pushed the raft up under an overhanging bank and held it fast until Hannah and I were ashore, then he and Faro followed us and we all stood and watched the raft drift away with the current.

"We'll eat now," said Big Eli, and Hannah opened the carpetbag and brought out cold chicken and biscuits and we ate our breakfast. I saw there was female riggin' in the bag too and guessed Hannah was aiming to stay a spell, where she was going.

Great water birds flew up and down the river and now and then one of them would dive and come up with a fish in his beak. A herd of deer came out on a sandbar to drink and when they caught our scent, the buck stood guard while the does and fawns quenched their thirst. Squirrels chattered in the leafy branches above us.

"You'd better catch a wink," Big Eli said to Hannah and me after we had finished eating. "I'll stand watch in case they followed us with dogs."

He rolled out the bear hide under a cypress and she slipped

off her boots and curled up. I lay down on the soft moss not far from her, but I had slept on Big Eli's shoulders while they traveled and I wasn't sleepy then. Soon Hannah was asleep and I lay there looking at her, wondering who she was and why she had run away with Big Eli and me. I would have asked Big Eli but I didn't want to wake her. He was sprawled on the riverbank with his eyes fixed on the other side, but now and then I caught him looking at her too and I wondered if he was thinking the same thoughts I had in mind.

It was past noon when he came and knelt down beside her. He reached out a hand and touched her on the shoulder. She didn't jump, but opened her eyes slow and looked about as if trying to make out where she was. When she saw me she smiled and sat up.

"We'll push on now," Big Eli said and stood up.

She put on her boots and we started off again through the woods, bearing to the north as we walked. Soon we came to a road that was almost as narrow as a trail and we followed it for almost two hours before we caught sight of the Tennessee. It was three times as wide as the Cumberland and not blue, but a muddy brown. It had me vexed, for I had seen the headwaters of both rivers in the mountains we had left a month before. There they flowed south. Here they were flowing north.

We stopped to rest and I asked Big Eli about it. He took a stick and traced their flow in the dust. Both started out in the mountains flowing south through Tennessee, he said, and then turned north to empty in the Ohio River. Then he pointed across the river.

"That's The Purchase over there," he said. "I reckon Humility's not far off."

Humility was the place where Uncle Zack and Aunt Soph lived.

We started walking again and in a few minutes the road ended at the river and I saw a man and a boat I knew to be a ferry. It was big enough to haul a wagon and team and had to be pulled across the river by a rope strung between trees, one on our side of the river and the other across it. Big Eli paid our tote with an otter hide he had brought along from The Gap, and the ferryman looked him over and asked, "Are you Zack Wakefield's brother?" Big Eli said he was.

"He told me to be on the look for you," said the ferryman, and he looked at Hannah. "He said there'd be two of you."

"There's three of us," said Big Eli.

"I can count," said the ferryman and grinned.

We went aboard and Big Eli helped him pull across the river and all the time the ferryman kept looking at Big Eli's long hair and broad shoulders. When we nosed into the landing, he said, "You don't favor your brother like a pea."

"I reckon not," said Big Eli, and I wondered what Uncle Zack looked like, for I didn't remember him.

The ferryman told us the direction to follow to Humility.

"You should fotch up there by supper time," he said. "Sophia Wakefield spreads a bounty of vittles."

We set off through a canebrake, but soon we came to timber again. There was a blue haze of smoke hanging over the country and I asked Big Eli if the forest was afire.

"No," he said, "it's folks clearing timber for new ground."

I looked at the trees so big and tall that they shut out the late afternoon sun and I reckoned that folks must want land mighty bad to go to the bother of clearing them away for ground to plough and seed. Soon we passed some new ground that had been cleared a year or so before and tobacco was growing in rows but it was different than the weed I had seen in Carolina and eastern Kentucky. The leaves were bigger and greener and looked heavier and I reckoned it must be the rich new land that made it different. Uncle Zack had said in the letter to Big Eli that someday The Purchase would grow more tobacco than the whole world set aside. That, I reckoned, was a heap of tobacco.

We got to Humility just at sundown, but we knew we were getting close to it before we saw it because the smell of supper was in the air.

There were a few log houses and a big barn built of sawed lumber, and supper smoke was rising from kitchen chimneys. As we got near the barn I saw a sign painted across the front of it. It read, "Zachariah Wakefield, Tobacco." It was Uncle Zack's barn, I knew. The houses looked all about alike except the one nearest the barn and it had a bay window of glass and I reckoned Uncle Zack was doing as well as he claimed in his letter.

The village dogs caught our scent and came barking toward us and I hung on to Faro's scruff to keep him from getting into a fight. People heard the ruckus and came to their doors to look out at us. A skinny man with a bald head came to the door of the house with the bay window in it. He looked at us and turned to call back in the house, "Sophia!"

I guessed that was Uncle Zack Wakefield and it was.

He stepped to the yard to meet us and Aunt Soph came out of the house, wiping flour on her apron. I reckoned Uncle Zack fed her well for she was pink and chubby. Uncle Zack shook hands with Big Eli and Aunt Soph grabbed me and we hugged and kissed until Faro thought she was mauling me and he started to growl and show his teeth. Then Uncle Zack and Aunt Soph looked at Hannah like they had just noticed she was with us.

"This is Hannah," said Big Eli.

"Hannah Bolen," said Hannah, and I remembered she hadn't told us her last name.

"She's looking for kin," said Big Eli.

"Adam Bolen," she said. "He's my uncle."

"Ever hear of him, Sophia?" Uncle Zack asked.

Aunt Soph shook her head. "So many folks have been coming into The Purchase since they cut the price of land from a dollar to fifty cents an acre, a body can't know them all," she said.

"We'll inquire tomorrow," said Uncle Zack and started to herd us into the house. "Supper's nigh ready."

Faro started to go in too but Uncle Zack shoved out a leg and stopped him. "Don't allow dogs in my house," he said and grinned at Big Eli and me. "Fleas make me scratch."

It was a large room with a fireplace as big as a corncrib and on one side of it was a secretary desk so tall it almost reached the rafters which were peeled walnut logs. He saw me looking at it.

"I hauled that from Carolina," he said, then looked at Big Eli and smiled proud. "And our granddaddy brought it from England in his day, eh Elias?"

Big Eli nodded. "So they tell," he said, and stacked the rifle at the other end of the fireplace. Then he unslung the Gabriel Horn from his shoulder and hung it on a peg beside the door.

"You'll want to wash up," said Aunt Soph to Hannah.

"Menfolks after," said Uncle Zack, and Hannah followed Aunt Soph to the kitchen. Big Eli and Uncle Zack sat down while I stood looking things over. Aside from several splint-bottom chairs, there was a bed covered with a quilt of many colors in the corner of the room and the tick on the bed looked so soft it made me sleepy. Next to it was a table with a turpentine lamp and a big Bible on it. Big Eli had told me that Uncle Zack was a pious man.

A door stood ajar and I could see into another room. It had a bed in it and I reckoned that's where Uncle Zack and Aunt Soph slept.

When Hannah had washed the travel dust off, Aunt Soph called Big Eli and me and she gave us soft soap and towels. While we washed, she and Hannah spread the vittles on the table and I remembered what the ferryman had said about her cooking. He knew what he was talking about. There was roast hog meat and stewed turkey with flat dumplings; roasted corn ears, hot pan bread as soft and fluffy as a feather bed tick, yellow yams and a tureen of steaming mulligatawny. In the center of the table was a mould of yellow butter shaped like a wooly lamb on a tomb rock. Two hot pies sizzled beside the oven. When I saw all the vittles I wondered why Uncle Zack was so skinny.

Aunt Soph called him to supper. He told Big Eli to sit on one side of the table beside me and he put Hannah across from us. Aunt Soph sat at one end where she would be close to the oven when it came pie time, and Uncle Zack sat at the other end of the table. He waited until Aunt Soph quit wiggling around, then he ducked his bald head over his plate and began to mumble the blessing. I was trying to make out his words when he finished sudden, looked up and said, "Pass the vittles, Sophia."

We were so hungry we let Uncle Zack do most of the talking and most of what he said was about himself. He told how he had come into The Purchase the day it opened for settlement and he had set up as a tobacco buyer.

"I let the other fellow clear the land and plant the weed," he said. "I'll buy it off him and ship it to New Orleans."

"He's done right well," said Aunt Soph.

Uncle Zack puffed out his chest. "We're comfortable," he said with a big smile.

Most of the time Aunt Soph just looked at Hannah and then Big Eli, like she wanted to ask questions but didn't dast. After supper Uncle Zack and Big Eli and I went into the big room while Aunt Soph and Hannah cleaned up the dishes. I could hear Aunt Soph and Hannah talking while they worked, but I couldn't hear what they were saying for the door between the rooms was partly closed. I guessed that Aunt Soph waited to get rid of us menfolks before she started asking questions and I wondered what Hannah was telling her, for she hadn't told us anything.

After a spell they came into the big room and Uncle Zack opened his Bible and read scripture. He was just closing the book when I heard Faro bark and a few seconds later there was a knock at the front door. Uncle Zack got up and opened it and I heard Hannah give a little scream and she started to cry. Then I saw who it was. It was Decker, the tavern keeper from Cadiz, and the Constable who had locked the wrist irons on Big Eli. Big Eli saw them too and he got up from his chair and edged over to where his rifle was stacked against the chimney.

"I'm an officer of the law," the Constable told Uncle Zack.

"We've come for him and her," said old Decker, pointing at Big Eli and Hannah.

Aunt Soph started to cluck like a hen on eggs.

"Come inside," said Uncle Zack and they did and he closed the door behind them. Old Decker and the Constable were keeping an eye on Big Eli and the rifle.

"We don't want any trouble," said the Constable.

"There won't be any if everything is legal," said Uncle Zack.

Hannah didn't stop crying, so I stood beside her and she took my hand and squeezed it hard.

"I'm a Squire," said Uncle Zack. "Tell me what this is about."

"Tell the Squire," said the Constable to old Decker.

Decker told how he had heard the nine blasts on the horn and had killed nine chickens, expecting that many customers to be on the stagecoach. He told how he and the others had put Big Eli into the smokehouse, expecting him to work out payment for the chickens. When he got that far, Uncle Zack stopped him.

"It ain't legal," he said. "You can't put a man in jail for debt unless a jury says he owes it."

"But he busted out of jail," said old Decker.

"He wasn't in jail legally in the first place," said Uncle Zack. "Bustin' out don't count."

"Then we'll arrest him for enticing a female indenture away from her master," said the Constable.

"I'm her master," said old Decker. "He stole her away from me."

Uncle Zack looked at Hannah and then at Big Eli.

"They didn't tell us she was a bound girl," he said. "I wouldn't have put her up if I'd have known it."

Decker told how Hannah was bound to him for four years and the contract still had a year to run. She was seventeen, he said, and that's what I had guessed she was.

Uncle Zack looked at Hannah. "Is that so, young woman?" he asked her and Hannah nodded her head that it was.

"We're taking her back," said Decker.

"And we're taking him back for enticing her away," said the Constable.

Aunt Soph hadn't said a word up to that time, but she began to cry and wring her hands. I thought it was because she was sorry for Hannah and Big Eli.

"Oh Zack," she wept, "it's a disgrace. What will folks say?"

Uncle Zack didn't get a chance to answer. Big Eli beat him to it.

"They're not taking us back to Cadiz," he said, looking at Hannah.

"Now Elias, hold your temper," said Uncle Zack. "If you and this female have broke the law, you'll have to pay the penalty."

"I know about indenture law," Big Eli said.

"He didn't entice me," Hannah said. "I ran off of my own free will."

Big Eli paid her no heed. "If a man entices a female indenture from her master, he's liable to law," he said, "but if he marries her, she's not bound by contract any more."

"That's the law," said Uncle Zack, "but you didn't marry her."

Big Eli shut him up. "I enticed her away and, by the will of God, I'm aiming to marry her!"

Aunt Soph began to sob. "What will folks say?" she said, and looked at Uncle Zack and shook her head. "What will they say?"

Uncle Zack got mad and waved his arms.

"You'll do nothing of the kind, Elias Wakefield," he shouted. "You didn't even know this female's name when you got here!"

"Don't cross me, Zack!" said Big Eli and he moved toward his brother. Uncle Zack backed up a pace and quieted down.

"It's disgraceful," said Aunt Soph and began blubbering again.

"You're a Squire," said Big Eli to Uncle Zack. "You can wed us."

The Constable shook his finger at Big Eli. "Marrying her won't clear you," he said. "We'll take you back for enticing."

I saw Uncle Zack stroking his chin and thinking hard. Something seemed to come to him for all of a sudden he sided with Big Eli.

"I think this can be fixed up betwix us," he said and smiled at the Constable and old Decker.

"How?" asked Decker.

"If you got paid for the time the girl has to work out, you'd be satisfied, wouldn't you?" he asked.

Decker thought it over. "The contract's got a year to run," he said.

"I'll pay it off," said Uncle Zack.

"But he's got to wed her," said the Constable, "and we're staying here until he does."

Big Eli turned to Hannah. "Are you willing?" he asked her.

Hannah looked at Aunt Soph, and I wondered why, but Aunt Soph didn't look at Hannah. She just flicked her nose like she smelled something she didn't like.

"I'll have to change my dress," said Hannah to Big Eli.

Aunt Soph had put the carpetbag in the bedroom and Hannah went in there and closed the door. Uncle Zack told old Decker and the Constable to sit down and take the weight off their soles and they did. Aunt Soph sat down too, but she looked at Big Eli and said, "You don't know this woman, Elias."

"She don't know me, neither," he said. "It's an even swap, I reckon."

I knew what Aunt Soph was thinking. She didn't think a bound girl was fit to marry a Wakefield.

Uncle Zack and old Decker were figuring out the money deal and drawing up a paper to make it legal. The clock on the mantel ticked on and it seemed to grow louder and louder as the seconds went by. When they got the deal down on paper Uncle Zack got a poke full of money from the tall secretary desk and looked at the clock, then turned to Aunt Soph.

"Is that female carding the warp and the woof for her bridal dress?" he asked, meaning Hannah was taking her time.

The Constable laughed. "She ain't sewing it with a red hot needle and a burning thread," he said.

"I'll fotch her," Aunt Soph said and got up from her chair. She opened the door to the bedroom and went inside, and I heard her scream, "She's gone!" She stepped back into the doorway with her eyes bugged out like she had seen a hant.

"She's not here!" she said.

Uncle Zack, old Decker and the Constable rushed to the bedroom to make sure for themselves, and Big Eli and I followed them. Aunt Soph was right. Hannah and the carpetbag were gone.

There was a door that opened into the yard and I knew she had gone that way. Uncle Zack ran outside followed by Decker, the Constable and Big Eli. Aunt Soph told me to stay with her. I could hear the men talking and Uncle Zack warning them to keep their voices down so the neighbors wouldn't hear. The voices faded away and I knew they were looking for Hannah, but it was dark and they didn't have a lantern. It was all of a half hour before they came back, but Hannah Bolen wasn't with them.

Uncle Zack got out his money again, counted some out and laid the paper he and Decker had drawn up under the light of the turpentine lamp. "Sign this," he said to Decker.

Decker signed his name and Uncle Zack handed him the money he had promised. "That pays off the indenture and squares everything," Uncle Zack said and Decker and the Constable nodded their heads.

Uncle Zack went to the front door and opened it.

"Now get out of here!" he yelled at them and Decker and the Constable hurried out and Uncle Zack slammed the door behind them. Then he turned to Big Eli.

"Elias," he said, "you owe me two hundred dollars."

"I'll work it out, Zack," said Big Eli.

Somehow I felt that Uncle Zack had tricked Big Eli into something, just like the biggety little stage driver had tricked him into blowing the Gabriel Horn on the Cadiz toll road.

"It's a blessing in disguise," Aunt Soph said, shaking her head and looking at Big Eli.

He didn't answer her, but sat down and shucked his boots. "We're tuckered," he said to Uncle Zack. "Where do we sleep?"

"The bed in the corner there," said Uncle Zack, and he yawned. "Sophia, let's retire," he said.

I must have been very tired for the sun was bright through the big bay window when I woke up the next morning. Big Eli wasn't in bed with me, and I could hear Uncle Zack and Aunt Soph talking in the kitchen. From what they said I knew he wasn't with them.

"Did you hear him get up?" I heard Aunt Soph ask Uncle Zack.

"No," he said. "He was gone when I got up."

"Where do you reckon he went?" she asked.

"Trackin' down that girl, I reckon," said Uncle Zack.

Aunt Soph chuckled. "Well Zack," she said, "you never ought to have written and asked your brother here."

I heard him blow his hot coffee. Then he said, "You leave Elias to me, Sophia. Since last night, I've got him where the hair's short. He won't cause us any more trouble."

"What if he finds that female and brings her here?" she asked.

"I'm betting he won't find her," he said. "She wasn't in such a hurry to get married. She wouldn't have cleared out of here so fast if she was."

Aunt Soph came to the door of the big room and I shut my eyes tight like I was still asleep. Then she went back to Uncle Zack and I heard them talking in low voices. I knew they didn't want me to hear what Aunt Soph was saying, but I caught a little of it, something about a woman named Miss Susie. It had something to do with what Aunt Soph and Hannah had to say when they were washing the dishes the night before. I wondered what it was and if it had anything to do with Hannah's running away after Big Eli offered to wed her.

Uncle Zack finished his breakfast and came into the big room. He was jolly when he saw me awake and called to Aunt Soph to put another skillet of eggs and hog meat on the coals. I got up and put on my riggin' and ate breakfast, then I went outside to look over the village.

Dogs growled and sniffed at me as I walked up the road, because I was a stranger. There was one store, about the size of Uncle Zack's big room, and a little farther on carpenters were laying a roof on a new tavern. In front of the tavern a crowd of boys and men were listening to a traveling herb peddler selling his cures. He had a lot of snakes in bottles but they were dead, pickled in alcohol. He had a lot to say about each snake and when he got through talking about them he started selling his wares. I was listening to him when I saw Big Eli and Faro come past the tavern. I ran to join them.

"Did you find her?" I asked him.

He looked at me like he was surprised that I knew what he had been doing and then he smiled, "No, I didn't," he said, and asked, "Did you want me to?"

"I hoped you would," I said.

He patted me on the shoulder. "Maybe we'll find her one of these days," he said.

That night I went to bed early, but not in the big room. Aunt Soph sent me to the room where she and Uncle Zack slept and I knew they were going to talk about things they didn't want me to hear. So I listened, though she closed the door thinking I couldn't hear what was said. Uncle Zack began to tell Big Eli what a fine country The Purchase was to live in and make money.

"I'm making money hand over fist, Elias," he said, "you can too if you'll settle down here."

"I'm not hankering to farm," I heard Big Eli say.

"Neither do I," said Uncle Zack. "I'm a business man, myself, and I can make one of you if you'll heed my teaching."

"You owe it to the boy," said Aunt Soph. "He should have a home and a mother, a good woman who will love him and teach him Godly ways."

"Sophia's right," said Uncle Zack.

"I reckon," said Big Eli. "I've only been putting it off."

"I'll teach you how to buy the weed," said Uncle Zack, "and I'll teach you how to grade and sell it. You can help me in the warehouse and learn while you labor."

"I'll have to work out the debt," Big Eli said.

I wondered what it would be like to see Big Eli working in a warehouse. He had never worked in my memory. All he had done was hunt and trap and fish. That wasn't easy, but it wasn't like working in a tobacco warehouse either. Uncle Zack would have thought our way of making a living was harder than buying and selling the weed.

"When will you be ready to start?" Uncle Zack asked.

"In a day or so," said Big Eli, and Uncle Zack waited a spell before he said anything.

"Going to look again for that female?" he asked.

I didn't hear Big Eli say anything.

"She's not for you, Elias," said Uncle Zack.

"If I can find her, I'll wed her," said Big Eli, and Aunt Soph and Uncle Zack didn't say anything more about Hannah. In a short spell Big Eli came to bed and I dropped off to sleep.

The next morning he was gone when I got up for breakfast and Faro was gone too, but the rifle and the Gabriel Horn had been left behind. I knew he wasn't hunting. He was looking for Hannah.

After breakfast I walked up to the tavern to watch the carpenters put on shingles. The herb peddler I had seen the day before had packed up his grip and was leaving in a wagon driven by a farmer. The team was heading toward the river. Some boys started poking fun at my long hair and I almost had a fight with one of them but when I pulled out my skinning knife and started playing mumblety-peg they let me alone. That afternoon I walked in the woods, which were deep and dark, and I found foot trails made by the Chickasaws before they sold their land to Andy Jackson and moved to Indian country in Mississippi. Wild turkeys called from the thickets and once, in the distance, a catamount screamed like a woman in pain.

Big Eli got home as Aunt Soph was putting supper on the table and I could tell by his face that he hadn't learned anything about Hannah or where she went.

Uncle Zack or Aunt Soph didn't mention her. Uncle Zack mumbled the blessing when we sat down to eat, and aside from that nothing worth the telling was said during the meal. When Big Eli finished eating he leaned back in his chair and looked at me for a long time like he was thinking of things he didn't want to say. Finally he turned to Uncle Zack.

"When do I start in the warehouse?" he asked.

"Tomorrow's as good a time as any," said Uncle Zack.

CHAPTER III

THE BUYING SEASON hadn't started, for most of the crop was in the fields, but Uncle Zack was getting ready for it. Stays and hoops for the hogsheads had to be shipped in by pole barge from Nashville and hauled by wagon from the river to Humility. They had to be put together in the warehouse and Uncle Zack hired two men to help out. The first day I watched the work go on and when the hogsheads were hooped and nailed together they were lined against the wall at the back of the warehouse. There were a lot of benches in the place and I wondered what they were for, but I didn't ask Uncle Zack for he was busy. It was after dark when he told the two hired men they could knock off and go home. He paid them in cash and then we went back to the house for supper.

We didn't go in the front door, but went to the kitchen to wash up before we ate. When we got inside, I saw that Aunt Soph had closed the door between the kitchen and the big room and when she saw me looking at it she put her fingers to her lips and whispered, "Don't go in there. Surprise!"

Big Eli looked puzzled but Uncle Zack cackled and nudged Aunt Soph with his elbow. While Big Eli and Uncle Zack washed up, I counted the chairs at the table and there were five of them and five plates had been set too.

Aunt Soph scrubbed my face and hands and took a comb out of her hair and ran it through mine, which hung down over my shoulders like Big Eli's. Uncle Zack shined his boots with a brush and so did Big Eli, though his didn't look as glossy as Uncle Zack's when he got through.

"Let me look you over," Aunt Soph said, and Uncle Zack lined me and Big Eli up beside him. "You'll do," she said, and went and opened the door between the kitchen and the big room.

"Come in, Miss Susie," she said.

A woman, medium tall and with hair as glossy black as a crow, appeared in the doorway. She was a young woman but older than Hannah, how much I couldn't guess. Her nose was thin at the bridge like Uncle Zack's, and she was wearing the prettiest dress I had ever seen. She stopped and looked at us, standing as straight as a Cherokee queen. She had a Sunday smile on her face.

Aunt Soph said, "Miss Susie, this is Zack's brother, Elias." Miss Susie smiled and tipped her forehead. Aunt Soph turned to Big Eli and said, "Elias, this is our good neighbor, Miss Susie Spann." Big Eli bowed and told Miss Susie he was glad to know her.

"Miss Susie keeps house for her brother," Uncle Zack said and I guessed she didn't have a man of her own. "He trades in slaves," Uncle Zack added.

Aunt Soph took Miss Susie's hand and led her into the kitchen. "They come from St. Louis," she said to Big Eli.

"Originally from New Orleans," Miss Susie said.

"We're from mountain country," Big Eli told her, and Miss Susie looked at me and smiled. Then she turned to Uncle Zack like she was surprised about something.

"Mister Wakefield," she said with a puzzled brow, "you told me your brother had a little son?" She and Uncle Zack and Aunt Soph laughed and I knew she meant that I looked like a girl because my hair was long.

"We haven't had time to cut off his hair," Uncle Zack said.

"After supper we'll attend to that," said Miss Susie.

I felt my eyes getting watery. "You won't cut off my hair," I said to her.

Uncle Zack roared laughing and Big Eli grinned, but he put a hand on my shoulder. "Miss Susie's joking," he said.

"The vittles will frost bite if you don't sit," Aunt Soph said.

Uncle Zack pulled back a chair for Miss Susie to sit in and motioned with his head for Big Eli to sit next to her. He put me in the chair beside Aunt Soph and he sat down at the head of the table as usual. We bowed and he blessed the vittles, the company and The Purchase. Instead of passing the vittles, Aunt Soph filled the plates and passed them around. While we ate, Uncle Zack did most of the talking and most of what he said was praising Aunt Soph's cooking.

"There's nothing like good vittles to make a man happy," he'd say and smile at Big Eli, and Aunt Soph would say, "But it takes a good man to provide the vittles," and she'd smile at Miss Susie.

After supper was over, Miss Susie offered to help Aunt Soph with the dishes but Aunt Soph wouldn't hear to it, saying Miss Susie might get dishwater on her dress. Aunt Soph asked me to dry the dishes instead, and Uncle Zack and Big Eli and Miss Susie went into the big room. When we had finished, Aunt Soph and I went in too and Aunt Soph asked me if I wasn't sleepy, but I said I wasn't and sat down next to Big Eli.

Uncle Zack didn't read Scripture that night. He and Aunt Soph kept asking and saying things that Miss Susie had to answer.

She told how she had lived in New Orleans as a girl and then when her folks died she went to St. Louis with her brother, Jim. They had moved to The Purchase when the Chickasaws moved out and settlers started moving in and taking over the new land. I got the feeling she didn't like The Purchase or most of the folks in it.

Then I heard Faro's deep bay about a mile away. I could tell by the pitch he'd struck a hot scent and I wished Big Eli and I were out on a ridge where we could hear him better. Big Eli got up from his chair and reached for the Gabriel Horn which was on the mantel, then he opened the door. I knew what he was going to do and I looked at Miss Susie who was watching him and wondering.

Big Eli didn't blow right off and I knew he was calculating the wind before he did and maybe giving Miss Susie plenty of time to get her ears set to hear him. Then he lifted the Gabriel Horn to his lips and the sound poured out like blue smoke from a gun muzzle, sharp as flint at first and then spreading out full and mellow to die far away on the light wind. It was as pretty a blow as I'd ever heard Big Eli do and I heard Faro skip a bay and I knew he'd caught it. It must have come unexpected to Miss Susie for she sat up straight with a jerk and looked from Uncle Zack to Aunt Soph, but she didn't say anything.

Big Eli shut the door and hung the Gabriel Horn on a peg next to the rifle and he looked a little disappointed that nobody mentioned the Gabriel Horn or Faro's hearing it. When he sat down Aunt Soph told me I should be in bed. I didn't want to shuck my riggin' with Miss Susie there, so I didn't budge from my chair.

In a spell Miss Susie said she'd have to go and Uncle Zack said, "Elias will carry you home," and he cackled, "He'll want to know which house it is so's he can find it again."

Aunt Soph frowned at him and said, "That's enough, Zachariah," and Miss Susie made like she hadn't heard a word of it.

While she was putting on her cape, Big Eli was standing there looking at her and she wasn't letting him miss anything for she turned slowly from Aunt Soph to Uncle Zack, telling them what a nice time she had and letting the lamplight shine full on her. Big Eli held out his arm and she took it and smiled up at him. He turned his head to see if I was watching and when he saw me grin, he reddened and said, "Better turn in, Little Eli."

They left and I began to get ready for bed. Aunt Soph and Uncle Zack seemed mighty pleased about everything.

"She'd make him a good woman," said Uncle Zack.

Aunt Soph nodded her head. "She's quality," she said.

I knew they were trying to make a match of their own whittling. I was asleep when Big Eli got home.

CHAPTER IV

A FEW DAYS later I heard Big Eli ask the two men Uncle Zack
had hired to help at the warehouse if they knew anybody by
the name of Bolen, Adam Bolen. They said they didn't. Hannah had said that was the name of her uncle who had come to
The Purchase. I guess Big Eli thought if he could find him he
could find Hannah. For two Sundays running he borrowed
one of Uncle Zack's horses and rode off without saying where
he was going, but I knew he was still looking for her.

Aunt Soph and Uncle Zack didn't like it because he missed
Sunday morning meeting which was held in Uncle Zack's
warehouse. The first Sunday I learned that the benches I
had seen were for folks to sit on when they came to hear
Uncle Zack read Scripture and preach. He wasn't a regular
preacher but they were scarce in The Purchase and until a
meetinghouse could be built the folks in Humility were willing to put up with him. After Big Eli had missed out on the
second Sunday, Miss Susie and her brother came over to
Uncle Zack's house one night.

She called him "brother" and he called her "sister." I had
seen him around the tavern a couple of times but I didn't
know he was her brother. I thought he was a gambler. He
wore a long black coat with tails, a fancy vest with a gold
watch chain across the front, and he sniffed snuff from his
thumbnail. He wasn't as tall as she was, but he wore high-
heeled boots to make up for it.

"Sister Susie tells me you're not a pious man," he said to Big
Eli.

Big Eli looked at Miss Susie. "What makes you think I'm
not?" he asked her.

"You don't go to meeting," she said.

Big Eli looked into the fireplace and didn't answer. He
had a way of doing that when he didn't want to talk about
something.

"A father should set a good example for his son," said Aunt Soph.

"He tells me Scriptures," I said, and asked if they wanted me to recite a psalm.

Miss Susie said she'd like to hear me, so I did.

When I got through, Uncle Zack said "Amen," and nodded his head. Big Eli looked at me and smiled like he was glad I took his side. Miss Susie said I did right well.

I guess Big Eli wanted to switch the subject for he asked Miss Susie's brother, "I hear you deal in blacks?"

Miss Susie's brother looked at him with a cocked, watery eye like he had just been raised in a card game and wasn't certain about calling the bet. "Yes," he said, "now and then."

"Business hasn't been what Brother Jim expected," said Miss Susie.

He took it up from there. "Nobody's got money to buy slaves," he said. "Not like in Mississippi and Louisiana where a man will have a hundred. Not like it at all."

"It's a different class of folks," said Miss Susie.

Brother Jim nodded. "They came in with an axe and a hoe, most of them did, and that's about all," he said. "Of course there're a few who can afford them and do, and some who can afford them and don't." He looked at Uncle Zack. "Zack Wakefield could use a couple with the way his business is growing," he added.

Uncle Zack fanned the toes of his boots like he was looking at himself in their shine. "I was thinking about buying one until Elias got here," he said. "Now I won't need any for a spell."

Big Eli was watching him as he said it. "You've come a far piece, Zack," he said.

Uncle Zack looked at him and asked, "In what way?"

"Recollect that dog you had when you and Soph got wed?" Big Eli asked him, and Uncle Zack nodded and said, "Yes?"

"Mighty good dog," Big Eli said. "Never ate his kill. Always brought it home to show how smart he was. If it was a rabbit you'd skin it and give him the hide and the guts. Then you and Soph would eat the meat."

I heard Aunt Soph start to cluck.

"Now you're talking about buying a slave," said Big Eli. "It's a far piece you've come."

Big Eli didn't believe in owning human beings or in trading in them. He thought it was a sin.

Aunt Soph went to the kitchen and Miss Susie followed her. Soon they came back with cake and pickles and passed them around. After we ate, Miss Susie and her brother went home, but I could see that Uncle Zack and Aunt Soph were vexed at Big Eli for what he had said.

The next Sunday Big Eli went to meeting. Uncle Zack stood at the door of the warehouse and shook hands with everybody like he hadn't seen them in a long time though he saw most of them every day.

He had sawed a hogshead in half to make a pulpit and when everybody got there he got up on it and led singing and then he said, "Let us pray." He got down on his knees, clasped his hands together and shut his eyes. Then he turned his face toward the rafters and prayed that the straying lamb be found and returned to the fold. He didn't have any sheep that I knew about and I guessed he must be talking about somebody else's sheep. When he got through praying he led another song. Aunt Soph knew the words but she needed practice on the tune. Miss Susie had a right pretty voice, a lot better than most of the other women. She had a hymn book and when she saw that Big Eli wasn't singing she leaned over against him and put the book in front of his face so he could read the words. I was glad, for Big Eli could sing. Many a night we had sat by the campfire and he'd sung to me, and other times when he'd come back to camp after dark, he'd start singing a mile away to let me know he was coming. Big Eli wet his lips with his tongue and joined in.

Miss Susie jerked up straight the way she did the night he blew the Gabriel Horn and everybody in the place turned to see who it was singing. I was real proud of Big Eli. I didn't have to listen to Aunt Soph for he drowned her out. Miss Susie quit singing. When the song was over she closed the hymn book and handed it to her brother and he kept it for the rest of the meeting.

Uncle Zack wasn't much of a preacher. He kept shouting until he ran out of words and then he'd read a passage of Scripture. That would start him off on another shouting spree and he'd yell and wave his arms like he was trying to scare Beelzebub out of the warehouse.

That wasn't the way I had learned the Scriptures from Big Eli. He never read Scriptures. He knew them by heart and at night he'd tell them to me and I'd get so excited I sometimes couldn't go smack to sleep when I slid under the bear hide. I'd lay there and look up into the night sky and it seemed to me I could see Little David winding up with his sling shot as old Goliath roared laughing at him and getting ready to draw back with his spear and hurl it at Little David like an Injun. Then, in my mind's eye, I'd see Little David, who wasn't scared at all, brace himself in his bare feet and let fly the rock with his sling shot and I could hear the rattle of iron as Old Goliath came tumbling down in his armor. I liked the Scripture about Little David.

And there was another Scripture about old King Pharaoh's daughter finding Little Moses. I never got tired listening to it for Big Eli would tell it right up to the place where she took Little Moses home in a basket and then Big Eli would ask me, "Do you know what she did?" and I'd say, "What did she do?" though I knew all the time what she did. Then Big Eli would say, "She yelled into the palace and said, 'Paw, come lookie what I found down yonder in that swamp!'" Then we'd both laugh. Uncle Zack didn't read Scripture like that.

One night I told the story of Moses to Miss Susie, but she didn't laugh when I finished, but I did. "You shouldn't laugh at Scripture," she said. "That is blasphemy." I still don't know what she thought was wrong with it.

That was the same night she asked Big Eli if he ever said blessing at table.

"Nobody asked me to," said Big Eli.

"Then I ask it," she said and looked at Uncle Zack to see

if he'd mind, and he didn't. Big Eli bent his face over his plate and shut his eyes, then began.

"God bless our vittles,
"God bless our shack,
"God bless Aunt Soph and Uncle Zack. Amen."

I knew he made up every word of it and I laughed. There was a twinkle in his eye when he looked up from his plate, but Miss Susie didn't smile. Her face just got red.

Aunt Soph looked at Big Eli and then at me and said, "Well!"

Uncle Zack tucked his napkin under his collar and said, "Pass the vittles."

CHAPTER V

WORK SLACKED OFF at the warehouse. The days were warm but sundown brought a chill to the air. One night, right after supper, Big Eli took the Gabriel Horn off the peg and said to me, "Let's have a run tonight."

He meant that Faro would do the running while he and I sat by a blaze on some ridge and listened to Faro bay after a fox. When we walked out of the house, Faro saw us and he must have seen the horn too for he began barking and jumping up on Big Eli. The moon was out and we headed into the hills overlooking the Tennessee. Wood smoke drifted like a light fog on the night air. Some of it came from timber that had been cut to make new ground but most of it came from tobacco barns where the new cut crop was being fire cured and it sweetened the air. Faro ran ahead of us, crashing this way and that through the thickets. A rabbit jumped up in front of him but he paid it no heed for Big Eli had taught him that only foxes were to be chased at night.

Big Eli and I walked along together saying nothing but I knew he was thinking the same things I was. It was the first time since we got to The Purchase that the three of us, counting Faro, had been alone together. We were enjoying it and there was no sense in talking about it.

Now and then Faro would yip, sometimes close and sometimes far away, and Big Eli would call out "Hock!" to let him know we were still with him. We had been walking about an hour when we saw from the top of a ridge a ribbon of silver winding through the valley below us. It was the Tennessee with the light of the moon shining on it. Big Eli halted and we stood there looking down on it for a long time, not saying a word. A deep bay from Faro broke the silence and I knew he had cut the scent of a fox about a mile away.

"Let's build a blaze," said Big Eli and both of us began gathering dry sticks and rotten limbs from the scrub timber that covered the ridge. By the time we had the fire started another voice joined Faro's in the chase. It was high pitched and excited.

"A bitch," said Big Eli when he heard it.

It wasn't long before another dog joined in with a medium pitch and the three of them faded into the far distance. The fire was blazing high, but soon it would bed down to glowing coals in which we could stare and dream. I heard something moving through the brush and dry leaves about a hundred yards away and recognized it as footsteps. A man wearing jeans gummy with tobacco, came into the rim of firelight. He and Big Eli howdied.

"Is that big-mouthed dog yours?" he asked, meaning the deep-pitched bay of Faro.

Big Eli said it was.

"Good dog," said the man. "That's my pup that joined in first."

"Sit down," said Big Eli, and the man hunkered to his haunches facing the fire, his elbows on his knees and his hands hanging limp in front of him.

"My name's Morgan," he said.

"Wakefield's mine," said Big Eli.

"I figgered," he said, looking at Big Eli's long hair and mine. "I hear you're from mountain country."

Big Eli said we were. Two other dogs had joined in to make a pack and it was running through a draw, the bays strong and paced for good running.

Another man appeared in the span of light.

"My brother, Anse," said Morgan. "Anse, this is Zack Wakefield's brother."

Big Eli and Anse Morgan nodded and howdied, then Anse looked at me. "Howdy, son," he said, and sat down by his brother. "Where's Tully and Bob?" he asked.

"They'll jine any time now," his brother said. "Their dogs are running."

Tully Morgan showed up with a jug of cider swung over his shoulder and a short time later Bob Morgan came in. He was younger than his brothers and was leading a big red hound that was heavy enough but its nose was a little too short and he held his tail out straight like a bird dog. Bob slipped the noose from the hound's neck and called, "Hock!" and the dog bounded into the bush in the direction of the running pack, but somehow he didn't seem to have his heart in it.

"Now you'll hear a fox race," said Bob Morgan with a proud grin. He sprawled down next to Big Eli, his boots poked toward the fire.

Tully Morgan uncorked the cider jug and passed it to Big Eli who tipped it over his wrist and took a swig and then handed it to me. I knew it must be sweet, not hard. I nipped it and passed it back to Tully Morgan. He took a swig and the jug was passed from brother to brother. They were all big men, except Bob, who had brought the dog, though he was medium height and weight. Anse Morgan, I guessed, was the oldest of the lot.

"How much you pay for that flea bait, Bob?" Anse asked his brother.

"A pretty shilling," Bob grinned.

"I hope he's worth his tote from Tennessee," said Anse, and his brothers laughed.

Bob told Big Eli that he had gone to Tennessee to buy the dog only the day before, and he wasn't shy about the red dog's breed. This started everybody off on tales about great dogs and great hunts and even Big Eli, who was mighty shy with strangers, told about some of the dogs he had owned and known about. Talk stopped only when the pack came near and then each of the brothers would try to pick out his own hound by the bay. Other hounds from other farms had joined in until there must have been more than a dozen in the race. Young Bob was certain that his red dog had taken the lead and was holding it. His brothers or Big Eli didn't dispute him.

The jug was passed again and dog talk went on. I had seen all of the brothers eyeing the Gabriel Horn from time to time and finally Bob said to Big Eli, "Mind if I look at your horn, Wakefield?"

Big Eli unslung it and handed it to him. The brothers

crowded close and fingered it like Injuns buying a blanket. They slid their fingers over the smooth surface, tapped it with hard fingernails to catch the pitch, and leveled it out in the firelight to admire its curve. Bob handed it back to Big Eli. Nobody said anything about it, but I knew they liked it and just didn't know what to say.

"Come here," said Tully, and Bob got up and walked over to where Tully was standing, looking into the bush. I saw Bob look into the bush too.

"That potlicker!" he yelled and swung his booted foot with all his might, and there was a yelp of pain and the red dog bounded into the light. Bob scrambled for a stick and threw it as the dog disappeared yelping into the dark.

The Morgan brothers screamed and yelled, rolled on the ground and slapped each other on the back, and Big Eli and I laughed too. Bob came back to the fire, picked up the cider jug and drained it.

"That potlicker!" he said, shaking his head. "While I'm bragging on him, he was asleep under that bush!"

I felt sorry for him as funny as it was.

About that time the pack made the kill a half mile below us. Big Eli put the Gabriel Horn to his lips and blew Faro in. The Morgan brothers looked at each other and nodded their heads and Tully Morgan said, "Mighty pretty music, Wakefield." They waited until Faro came bounding in, his long red tongue hanging out and dripping slobber. Big Eli stanced him so they could see what a good dog he was and the brothers went over him inch by inch. They fingered his loose mouth, lifted his wide feet and felt them, took note of the tilt of his tail.

"He's all of his bay," said Anse Morgan. "I'd admire a litter out of my bitch by him."

Big Eli said we'd better be going and the Morgans asked us to come back again and we said we would and then Big Eli and I headed toward Humility. Daybreak was greying the sky behind us as we came up to Uncle Zack's house. Smoke was threading out of the kitchen chimney and the smell of frying hog meat was in the air.

At breakfast we told Aunt Soph and Uncle Zack where we had been and who we had met.

"They're good farmers," said Uncle Zack, "but keep friends with them. You never want them against you."

"I figgered," said Big Eli.

"They stick as close as cotton seed," said Uncle Zack, "and I reckon the only one who hasn't killed a man in his day is young Bob."

"I figgered," said Big Eli.

CHAPTER VI

IN MID JULY Aunt Soph had heard a cricket in the kitchen woodbox. "Sixty days and we'll have frost," she had said to me.

In the days that passed, I forgot about it. The leaves began turning and the hills looked like a crazy quilt of color. Swarms of canaries, yellow and tinged with green, began gathering and parakeets chattered in the hazel thickets before winging south. One morning, right after I had seen two V's of geese flying a mile high over Humility, I went into the back yard to split kindling for the kitchen and there was frost on the axe. I rushed back into the house to tell Aunt Soph that she was right about the cricket she had heard in July.

Uncle Zack was standing in front of the kitchen fireplace warming his rear and working up an appetite for a skillet of squirrels Big Eli had shot at daybreak.

"Two years ago this time the passengers came," he said.

"What's that?" I asked him.

"Pigeons," he said. "Wild pigeons."

I had seen a few in the Cumberlands but not many, and with all the birds except jays, crows, hawks and owls heading south for the winter, I wondered why he bothered to mention pigeons. By the time we ate breakfast I had forgotten all about what he had said. He and Big Eli had some odd jobs to do in the warehouse and I went with them to play fort and Injuns in the big hogsheads that were to be filled with tobacco when the season came around and Uncle Zack started buying. That afternoon I took Faro and went into the woods to pick hazelnuts and look for muscadines.

It was getting close to sundown when I heard it, and I wouldn't have paid much attention except that Faro cocked his head and listened, then bristled and began to whine like he was afraid. Faro wasn't afraid of anything unless it was

43

something he didn't understand or had never seen before. That's why I was afraid. It sounded like a storm coming in fast from the north. We broke and ran for Humility and as we raced around the warehouse I saw people running out of houses and looking up at the sky to the north. Uncle Zack, a hammer in his hand, came running out of the warehouse with Big Eli right behind him.

"A hurricane," I yelled, because the sky had darkened to the northwest and the roar was getting louder by the second.

Uncle Zack dropped his hammer in the dust and pointed.

"It's the passengers!" he shouted to make himself heard.

Faro started to howl, and then I saw them coming in.

"There's millions of them!" shouted Uncle Zack.

I didn't know how much a million tallied, but I guessed he was right for I didn't believe there were so many birds in all the world, including bluejays and crows. They came in low clouds and swarmed around the village and then they'd see the people standing in the road and they would swoop high again and swirl around like a cyclone twister. The sky got black as night. After a while they began swooping into the timber at the west end of the village and I heard limbs cracking under their weight. Nobody tried to talk because of the noise they made, and it didn't quiet down until long after real dark set in by the clock. Even then, I could hear them passing over and there were no stars in the sky.

There wasn't a supper cooked in the village that night; men and women and children and dogs started coming into Humility long before the roar of the passengers overhead had stopped. They came on foot, on mule and horseback, in wagons and rigs. Some brought scatter guns, some had rifles, and others cut long poles after they got there. Bonfires were built along the road and guns began booming all through the woods and the men with the long poles beat the lower limbs of the trees. The women and children ran about with lanterns, picking up dead pigeons and stuffing them in tow sacks or throwing them in wagon beds, for the ground was littered with them. Uncle Zack didn't kill any himself, but he and Aunt Soph picked them up by the armful. Big Eli and I just watched, and then I got a look at his face and it was hard to tell whether he was scared or killing mad.

He was watching a man about the size of himself who carried a twin barreled muzzle-loader and a whiskey jug. The man would stand off and fire both barrels into the trees and watch birds rain down from the limbs, then he'd reload and take a swig from the jug and start over again. Not once did he pick up his kill, and he kept at it for an hour. After a while he came to the bonfire where we were standing and began to swab his gun with a ramrod. Sweat was running down his face like he had just climbed out of a creek. He looked at us with a big grin.

"Where's your gun, Mister?" he yelled at Big Eli, and reached for his powder horn which was a long one with silver tip and ornament.

Big Eli didn't answer him. He just walked over, took hold of the powder horn like he was admiring how pretty it was.

The man must have thought that was what Big Eli was doing for he didn't object, and then I saw Big Eli tip the horn and the powder poured out on the ground. The man was so surprised at what he saw that he tried, but couldn't talk.

"You've done enough shooting for tonight," Big Eli said, and handed the horn to him. Then he came back to me, took my hand and we started toward Uncle Zack's house.

We had just got inside and lit a candle when Uncle Zack and Aunt Soph came in with two tow sacks filled with pigeons which they dropped to the floor and shut the door. I could see they were upset about something.

"It's a good thing you emptied that powder horn complete," said Uncle Zack to Big Eli.

"Why?" asked Big Eli.

"That's Stan Bodine," Uncle Zack said. "He's a bad man to cross. He'd have shot you if you'd left him the powder to do it."

"He's a whiskey rebel from Pennsylvania," said Aunt Soph.

Big Eli didn't seem interested. He began to shuck his boots and get ready for bed.

Just before daybreak I heard the pigeons breaking roost and taking wing. For a while they roared overhead like they had the night before, and then everything got quiet except for the noise Uncle Zack made in chunking up the kitchen fire for breakfast. Aunt Soph got up too and I heard them plucking pigeons for an hour before they started breakfast.

When Big Eli and I got up, Aunt Soph had two skillets on the coals and they were filled with birds stewing in their own fat, but I couldn't look at them and I wondered what I'd do when she filled my plate. Big Eli finished his ablutions and then he went to the potrack and took down a big skillet. He looked at me and saw how green I was.

"Ham or pigeons?" he asked.

"Ham," I said.

He cut two slices, put them in the skillet and set it on the coals. He must have been sick at his stomach too.

During the day more people came to Humility to pick up pigeons that had been killed the night before and they took them away in sacks and wagons, but when they had gone the ground was still littered with hundreds of dead birds.

In about a week the stink got so bad in the face of a west wind that the men in the village had to dig a trench and bury them. Big Eli didn't help them.

"Do you want to go fox hunting with the Morgans to-night?" he asked me.

I said I did, and then I remembered I hadn't seen a Morgan the night the passengers came over. They were hunting men. Not potshooters.

CHAPTER VII

Long before we reached the ridge that overlooked the river, Big Eli blew a couple of blasts on the Gabriel Horn. Faro had been running well ahead of us and he heard it and came bounding in. Big Eli had to "Hock!" him out again, and it wasn't long before we could hear him and a couple of the Morgan dogs hot on a scent in the valley below us.

Anse and Tully Morgan were waiting for us, for they had heard the Gabriel Horn too. They had a blaze started and there were two jugs of cider instead of one. Anse saw me looking at them and he said, "The one with the cob stopper is for you, Little Eli," and he was grinning when he said it.

"Who's the other one for?" I asked.

"For us grownups," he said and chuckled. "It turned hard as a mule's kick last week."

The other brothers came in shortly and more dogs joined in the run, but talk at first was about the passenger pigeons and not dogs. They had heard about Big Eli's dumping Stan Bodine's powder horn.

"It's time somebody emptied it for him," Anse said.

His brothers agreed. "But he'll get square," said young Bob. His brothers agreed to that too.

"He'll shoot you when you're not looking," said Tully. "If I were you, Wakefield, I'd find a way to cross him. Then I'd kill him."

Big Eli didn't look up. He just stared into the fire for a few seconds before he answered. "I don't hanker to kill no man," he said.

The Morgans looked at each other and said no more about Stan Bodine. Somehow I got the feeling they thought that if Big Eli had to kill a man he'd do it.

Tully Morgan reached for the jug of hard cider and passed it to Big Eli. "Have a drink," he said, and Big Eli tipped it to his lips and swigged.

47

I uncorked my jug and drank too. The dogs were running good by then and their voices were as mixed as the colors on a crazy quilt and just as pretty. For a long time we listened as the jug of hard cider was passed around again and again.

"I hear you sing?" said young Bob, looking at Big Eli with a grin.

Big Eli smiled sly like and said, "You have good ears."

Everybody laughed at that, because they had heard about Big Eli's busting up the singing at Uncle Zack's Scripture meeting. But Big Eli was making like he thought Bob had heard him all the way from Humility to the valley of the Tennessee.

"Little Eli, can you sing?" Tully Morgan asked me and I said I could if I knew the tune.

"You know this one," he said, and started singing *Possum Up a Gum Tree*, which was General Andy Jackson's favorite piece. Bob Morgan took another swig from the jug and yelled, "Join in!" and we all did. The jug kept going around and we sang more songs and I saw a sparkle in Big Eli's eyes I had never seen before.

Meanwhile the voices of the pack kept fading in and out as they came near the ridge and then wound down through the draws. It was about the prettiest music I had ever heard.

Terry Morgan hefted the cider jug and shook it to see how much was left and instead of taking a swig he held it toward Big Eli. "Take what the shoemaker threw at his wife," he said, meaning it was the last, but Big Eli shook his head.

"I've had enough," he said.

Terry tipped the jug and let the cider run out on the ground, what there was of it. "Then let's give it to the gods," he said, and I wondered what he meant.

"Do you dance?" young Bob asked Big Eli, and I wondered if he had hefted the jug too often.

"I can," said Big Eli.

Bob said the Morgans were having a dance Saturday night and he wondered if Big Eli would like to come. Big Eli didn't have a chance to say whether he would or he wouldn't. Terry butted in and said to young Bob, "If your girl ever gets a look at him and that long hair of his'n, you'll be dancing by your-self."

The brothers laughed, agreeing with Terry. Young Bob looked at Big Eli like maybe his brothers were right about what Terry had said.

"I never stole a mare out of the shafts yet," said Big Eli, which meant he wouldn't try to take another man's girl.

"I believe you," said Bob. "We'll be expecting you Satur-day night."

Anse Morgan yawned and said they had better be going, but Tully had gone to sleep on the ground and his brothers had to rough him up to get him awake. Big Eli blew the Ga-briel Horn for Faro to come in though the pack was running hot. The Morgans didn't wait, but started down the ridge and Tully and Bob were reeling a little and singing *Old Dan Tucker* out of tune.

When Faro came in, Big Eli squatted down and said "Climb up," and I got on his back. I didn't remember getting back to Uncle Zack's or having gone to bed when I did.

CHAPTER VIII

Big Eli had worked out about half of what he owed to Uncle Zack and figgered he could pay off the other half when tobacco came in season and Uncle Zack started buying. We hadn't paid any board, but Big Eli was paying our keep with game he shot and put on the table and the odd jobs I did about the place. But we didn't have any cash in hand and we both needed things like new boots for me and a hat and jeans for Big Eli. He hadn't mentioned the dance the Morgans were giving on Saturday night and I guessed he wasn't going because he didn't have riggin' fit to wear. He was almost twice the size of Uncle Zack so he couldn't wear any of his hand-me-downs, and yet I knew he would like to go to the dance though he hadn't said so.

It was about noon and Big Eli and Uncle Zack had come in to eat, but Aunt Soph hadn't put the vittles on the table and they were sitting in the big room waiting. I was sitting in the open door whittling sticks when I heard a horse coming up the road but I didn't pay attention until I heard a man's voice say "Whoa!" in front of our house. I looked up to see who it was and my heart skipped a beat and my tongue got so dry I couldn't speak. Uncle Zack must have heard the horse and saw me getting up, for he asked, "Who is it, Little Eli?"

"It's him," I said. "Stan Bodine!"

Uncle Zack jumped out of his chair like he had sat on a hornet. "He's here for trouble, Elias!" he said to Big Eli. Aunt Soph heard him and came to the kitchen door with a pan of hot biscuits in her hands.

"Don't let him in, Zack," she said.

Big Eli got out of his chair and walked toward the front door. "I'll see what he wants," he said. He stopped square in the door, his hands on his hips.

Bodine saw him and stopped. He looked at Big Eli like he

had never laid eyes on him before. "I want to see Squire Wakefield," he said.

Big Eli stepped aside. "Come in," he said, and then he faced Uncle Zack. "He wants to see you, Zack."

"Howdy, Squire," said Bodine when he came in and Uncle Zack mumbled something and shook his head. Bodine saw Aunt Soph and took off his hat. Big Eli went back to his chair and sat down, and Uncle Zack pointed to a chair and said to Bodine, "Won't you sit?" Bodine did, but he didn't waste any time getting to what he came for.

"I understand you paid indenture for a bound girl named Hannah Bolen," he said.

I heard Aunt Soph cluck. Uncle Zack cleared his throat and said, "Yes, I did, Bodine." Then he named the amount he had paid.

Bodine stiffened his right leg and shoved his hand into his pants pocket. He drew out a long purse made out of a doe's tail and which had a silver snap on it. "I want to pay it off," he said.

Uncle Zack looked at Big Eli who was looking at Bodine. Bodine was counting out money, some silver and some paper.

"I'll write a receipt," Uncle Zack said and went to his secretary desk.

Aunt Soph stepped back into the kitchen to put the pan of biscuits on the table but she was back in time to see Bodine hand the money to Uncle Zack. I was wondering how Bodine knew about Hannah's being a bound girl and how he knew that Uncle Zack had paid off the indenture. I looked at Big Eli and knew he was wondering about the same thing as well as why Bodine was paying it off. Uncle Zack handed Bodine the receipt and Bodine put it in his purse and shoved the purse into his pocket. Then he got up to leave and Big Eli got up from his chair too. I saw Aunt Soph's hands start to trembling and she clucked a couple of times for she was wondering what Big Eli was going to do and so was I.

"Are you her kin?" Big Eli asked Bodine.

There was a grin on Bodine's lips. "No, I'm not her kin," he said. "I'm her husband."

He stood looking at Big Eli like he was waiting to tell more if anybody asked him, but Big Eli didn't say anything and Bodine turned toward the door. "Obliged to you, Squire," he said, and went out to his horse. When he heard the horse trot up the road, Uncle Zack fingered the money Bodine had given him and which he still held in his hand, and said to Big Eli, "Elias, I guess I owe you money now."

Big Eli nodded. "You can pay me now," he said.

Uncle Zack went to his secretary desk and figured on paper for a few seconds or so. After he tallied up how much of the indenture Big Eli had worked out, he counted the difference in cash and handed it to him.

"We're square, Zack," said Big Eli and pocketed it.

Aunt Soph said the vittles were on the table and we went in to eat and except for the blessing which Uncle Zack mumbled over his plate, there wasn't a word said until Big Eli finished his snack. He shoved back his chair like he was going to get up.

"Zack, I'd like the loan of a mule for a couple of days," he said.

Uncle Zack nodded his head. "Catch up the one you want any time you want it," he said.

Big Eli went into the big room and got his hat and when he came back through the kitchen he let his hand fall on my shoulder. "Take care of Aunt Soph and Uncle Zack," he said, and went to the stables. A few minutes later I watched him jog up the road in the direction Stan Bodine had taken, but the rifle was still by the fireplace and I reckoned he wasn't hunting trouble. From the kitchen I heard Aunt Soph and Uncle Zack talking.

"Where do you reckon he's gone?" Aunt Soph asked.

"No telling," said Uncle Zack. "Elias was always like that. Let something happen he didn't like and he'd disappear for days at a time. Sometimes weeks or a month."

"Yes, I know," said Aunt Soph, and then they were quiet for a spell.

After a while Uncle Zack said, "I hope he's learned his lesson," and I knew he was talking about Big Eli's wanting to marry Hannah Bolen.

"It's a blessing in disguise," said Aunt Soph.

But I didn't feel like they did about it. All I knew was that I hated Stan Bodine and I wanted to hate Hannah for marrying him, but I couldn't and I knew I never would. I wondered if Big Eli felt the same way I did and if that was why he rode off on Uncle Zack's mule. Faro was asleep in the shade of a sycamore in the back yard. I called him and we headed into the woods to hunt Chickasaw trails.

CHAPTER IX

Two DAYS passed and Big Eli didn't come home and by Saturday noon I guessed he had forgotten all about the dance at the Morgans'. Then along about the middle of the afternoon I saw a long-eared mule coming down the road and Big Eli was astride him. I whistled and Big Eli waved a hand at me and Faro saw him and dashed off to meet him. I could see there was a lot of truck tied to the saddle, but as he came up to me he reached out a hand and lifted me up in front of him. He let the mule have his head and he put his arms around me and held me tight. Uncle Zack and Aunt Soph were standing in the door watching us. Big Eli pulled up the mule. He slipped me to the ground and got off the mule and then began untying the truck from the saddle. They were wrapped in brown paper and smelled like a store.

"What's in them?" I asked him.

"A surprise," he said with a big grin on his face.

As we came to the door, Aunt Soph looked at him with a grin and asked, "Who trimmed your hair?"

I hadn't noticed it until then, but she was right. It didn't look any shorter but it was smooth around the sides and somebody had used a razor around his ears. And then I smelled honeysuckle. Aunt Soph must have got a whiff of it. She sniffed her nose and asked, "Elias, have you been drinking?"

Big Eli grinned and bent down and kissed her smack on the mouth, giving her a chance to smell his breath.

"He's acting like it," said Uncle Zack.

"Tain't so," Aunt Soph laughed. "It's only on his hair and not on his breath."

Big Eli laughed out loud and we all followed him into the house. He tossed his hat on the hook and then he handed me a bundle and said, "Open it." He gave me his pocketknife to cut the cord. I was so excited I almost cut my hand and Uncle Zack wanted to help me but I wouldn't let him. It was a pair of boots, glossy black with rawhide straps to lift them by. I kicked off the ones I was wearing and slipped my feet into the new ones and the air seemed full of the smell of new leather. I couldn't say anything because I didn't know what to say.

"How much they cost you, Elias?" Uncle Zack asked.

Big Eli didn't answer him. He picked up another bundle and gave it to Aunt Soph and she looked at him and asked, "For me?" like she never had a present given to her before. Big Eli clipped the cord, for her hands were shaking, like they had the palsy. She ripped the paper away.

"A new dress!" she said, and held it up for us to see. "Made of bombazine, too!"

It rustled like dry leaves in the fall and she spread it out against her front like she was wearing it and she nearly lost her breath when she saw how low it was cut in front.

"Made in New Orleans," said Big Eli.

Uncle Zack shook his head and squinched his lips. "A fool and his money's soon parted," he said.

Aunt Soph hugged and kissed Big Eli. "Pay no heed to what he says," she said, and Big Eli laughed and reached for another package that had not been opened. He handed it to Uncle Zack.

"Just in case you get snake bit, Zack," he said with a grin.

Uncle Zack tore off the wrapper and held out a demijohn that had a net of straw around it.

"French brandy," said Uncle Zack and smacked his lips.

Aunt Soph grabbed my hand and also Uncle Zack's and the three of us danced a ring around Big Eli and laughed and when we quit, he said, "I've got to wash off. I smell of mule."

Aunt Soph hurried into the kitchen to get out the wooden wash tub and I heard her ladling hot water from a pot on the coals. Big Eli followed her and carried two bundles he hadn't opened. Then he shut the door, leaving Uncle Zack and me in the big room. In a few minutes Aunt Soph came out and she was all smiles. She picked up her new dress and wrapped it in the paper it came in. "I've got to show it to Miss Susie," she said and dashed out the front door. Soon I could hear Big Eli splashing around in the tub but I was so excited about my new boots I forgot all about him until Aunt Soph came back from Miss Susie's house.

"Is he still in there?" she asked. Just then the door opened and Big Eli stepped through, only I wasn't certain it was him. He was in new riggin' from Wellington boots to a broad-brimmed beaver like Pennsylvania keelboaters wore. His jeans had stripes in them and covered the tops of his boots to sag a little at the bottom. But the coat was the biggest surprise of all. It was made of black cloth, with black buttons on the sides, and it puckered like a wasp at the waist. His long yellow hair rolled over the collar like butter off a hot ear of corn.

I thought Aunt Soph was going to kiss him. Uncle Zack looked him over and said, "All dressed up and no place to go."

"How about it, Sophia?" Big Eli asked.

"Zack's wrong," she said, then turned to Uncle Zack. "He's carrying Miss Susie to the Morgan dance tonight."

Then I knew why Big Eli had shut the door when he and Aunt Soph went into the kitchen and why she had hustled over to see Miss Susie.

Uncle Zack began rubbing his hands together like a raccoon washing beetles. "Then I'd wager you'd hanker the loan of my rig and team," he said to Big Eli.

"I'd admire to, Zack," Big Eli said.

CHAPTER X

UNCLE ZACK wouldn't let Big Eli hitch the team because he would smell of horses if he did. We caught out the chestnut filly and the roan gelding with a blaze face and then we groomed them until they were as glossy as my new boots. After that we got the harness and rubbed it clean with bear grease, and then hitched the team to the rig. The horses were never worked and in the chill fall air their spirits tickled them like a burr under their cruppers. They were stepping high when I opened the lot gate and the rig rolled into the road with Big Eli handling the reins. It was starting to get dark and candle lights were shining through the windows in the village. Doors began to open and neighbors watched as Big Eli made a wide turn and reined in at Miss Susie's. She must have been waiting for him for she came out with her brother. Big Eli touched the brim of his new beaver and stepped out of the rig. I saw him hist her into the seat and then climb in beside her.

Aunt Soph called from the doorway to Uncle Zack and me.

"Don't strain your eyes," she said.

The rig rolled by and Miss Susie waved a handkerchief at Aunt Soph and Aunt Soph waved at Miss Susie. It was too dark to see what Miss Susie looked like in her dancing finery but in my mind's eye it wasn't her sitting up there with Big Eli and it wasn't Big Eli sitting there with her. It was Hannah Bolen and me and she smelled as sweet as a posy and I was wearing a long black coat and a keelboater's beaver.

We went inside. A fire was blazing in the fireplace and I took off my new boots and set them where the light could flicker on them. Aunt Soph got out her new dress that Big Eli had brought to her and began sewing lace around the neck so it wouldn't look so low cut when she wore it. Uncle Zack uncorked his brandy and sucked a mouth full, then smacked his lips and put the demijohn back on the shelf in the corner. Next he read Scripture for a while and then I climbed into bed and went to sleep. I don't know when or why I woke up again but Aunt Soph and Uncle Zack were still sitting by the fire and they were talking low so as not to wake me.

"She's a lady and would make a good mother for the boy," Aunt Soph was saying.

Uncle Zack agreed and then he asked, "Do you reckon she's warming to him, Sophia?"

"It's too early to tell with a woman like her," said Aunt Soph. "She's not like the riffraff he's trucked with before."

"Seems to me she's not clabbered to him the way I fancied she would," Uncle Zack said.

"You talked him up so much before he got here, maybe the telling was sweeter than the smelling," said Aunt Soph.

"I know," said Uncle Zack. "You wouldn't have said anything about him at all and when he got here Miss Susie would have swooned. I know. I know."

They were silent for a while.

"Too bad he couldn't get her like he did Dolly," Uncle Zack said, and I knew he was talking about my mother who I didn't remember ever seeing.

"Zachariah!" Aunt Soph sounded indignant.

Uncle Zack chuckled. "There's more than one way of getting a woman," he said.

He got up and stretched his arms and yawned. "Bedtime, Sophia," he said and began banking the coals with ashes.

She went to their room and he followed her and soon I heard him snoring. I lay there wondering about what they had said and wondering if I should ask Big Eli what they meant but I decided not to. I understood enough to know that Dolly was not like Miss Susie and I wondered if she was like Hannah Bolen. Big Eli had never talked about Dolly except to say when I asked him one time that she had died soon after I was born. I dropped off to sleep but woke up again when Big Eli climbed into bed. I made like I was asleep for I knew he was tired from dancing most of the night, but I wouldn't have been able to sleep much for he kept rolling and tossing. That wasn't like Big Eli. He usually slept as dead as a poled ox. I got up at daybreak and chunked the fire in the kitchen to have it ready for Aunt Soph when she started breakfast.

CHAPTER XI

Most of the leaves had fallen and the sweet smell of tobacco curing in the barns was no longer in the crisp air. It was then that Uncle Zack started buying and Big Eli and I went along with him. We rode Uncle Zack's two mules, me up behind Big Eli, and we would leave before daybreak and wouldn't get back until after dark.

We would ride up to a farmhouse and light when the farmer came out. He and Uncle Zack would talk a while about happenings and then we'd go to the farmer's barn and the farmer would climb up the rafters and hand down a few sticks of tobacco for Uncle Zack to look at. The leaves had not been stripped from the stalks, which were split almost to the end so they could straddle the sticks. Uncle Zack would finger the leaves like a woman buying silk and hold them out to judge their length and weight. Then he'd hand back the tobacco, squint his eyes like he was calculating and make a bid. Sometimes the farmer would nod his head and take the price Uncle Zack offered. Sometimes he wouldn't. If he did, Uncle Zack would give him a few dollars to seal the bargain. The farmer would get the balance when he delivered the crop. No papers were signed. They just took each other's word and Uncle Zack never wrote down the price he had promised to pay because he kept it in his head and never forgot it.

Sometimes after he had made a bid, he would have to dicker because Tennessee buyers had offered more. When he did, it always made him mad.

"I wish those Tennessee buyers would stay out of my bailiwick," he'd say when we rode out of earshot of the farmer.

Uncle Zack had a lot of tricks.

He jollied the children and felt little boys' muscles to see how strong they were. If we were invited to eat with the farmer and his family, he bragged on the woman's cooking. After he ate he would say to the woman, "My Sophia told me to ask if you could spare her a planting of beans."

That pleased the farmer's wife and he got the beans. Then the next day, if we were invited to eat at another farm, he would give the same beans to the farmer's wife and say, "My wife, Sophia, told me to give you these beans for seed." That made her feel good and it put the farmer in a good humor when we went to the barn to bid on his crop.

Big Eli heard him do this many times before he said anything about it. Finally he said, "Zack, you ought to run for office. You're as two-faced as a politician."

Uncle Zack laughed. "Now you're learning how to buy tobacco," he said.

New farms had opened up since Uncle Zack had bought the year before and he didn't want to miss any of them. He would ask about new settlers when we stopped at farms. We had been out about a week when we stopped at a place late one afternoon and after he had bid on the crop he pointed to a thread of smoke rising over the forest about three miles away.

"Who lives over yonder?" he asked the farmer.

"Fella named Bodine," said the farmer. "Moved in about six months or so ago."

Big Eli looked at me but he didn't let on that he knew who the farmer was talking about. Uncle Zack nodded his head and said, "Bodine don't grow the weed."

The farmer smiled. "And that smoke you see ain't coming from his barn," he said. "It's coming from his still. He starts firing about this time of evening."

We got on our mules and rode back to Humility.

That night it started raining, slow but steady like it might keep up for a long spell. Uncle Zack listened to it drumming on the kitchen roof like it was music he hankered to hear.

"They'll start stripping now," he said, meaning that the rain would bring the tobacco leaves in order, making them soft as doeskin, and the growers would begin stripping them from the stalks and tying them into hands ready for delivery at the warehouse.

CHAPTER XII

THE RAINS kept up off and on for a week, sometimes driving hard and then slackening off to a cold drizzle. Uncle Zack and Big Eli spent most of the time at the warehouse getting things in shape for the farmers when they started delivering the crop. The road through the village turned into a river of mud, churned up by the teams and wagons that passed. I put away my new boots that Big Eli had bought for me and put on the old ones.

The rains stopped and the cold snap came. One morning when I got up there was ice on the waterbucket in the kitchen and when I went outside to get kindling, the ground was frozen hard. Late that day it began to snow but soon after dark it stopped, leaving a rising raw wind whining like a ghost through the trees and around the eaves of the houses and Uncle Zack's warehouse. Big Eli came home at suppertime and said that Uncle Zack had gone to hire a couple of hands to help unload the wagons when deliveries started. We were eating supper when he came in and after he had washed he sat down at the table, said blessing, though Big Eli had already done it, and Aunt Soph ladled up his plate.

"They'll start rolling tonight," he said to Aunt Soph, and then he asked her, "Has Conse Foster been around?"

Aunt Soph said that she hadn't seen him and about that time there was a knock at the front door and she went to answer it.

"Here he is now," she called to Uncle Zack, and then I heard her say, "Come in, Sheriff."

Uncle Zack got up and shook hands with him and then introduced Big Eli.

"Is Zack making a tobacco man out of you?" the Sheriff asked Big Eli.

"He's aiming to," Big Eli said.

"He's learning fast," Uncle Zack said, shaking his head like he was proud of what he had taught Big Eli.

There was a sly grin on the Sheriff's face when he asked Big Eli, "Has Zack showed you how to hide rocks in the scales?"

"Not yet," said Big Eli.

"Then you've still got a lot to learn from him," said the Sheriff and laughed. Uncle Zack laughed too and slapped the Sheriff on the back.

Aunt Soph spread a plate in front of the Sheriff and he set to. He was a man medium tall and though he looked skinny, his muscles were as tough as the rim of a wagon wheel. His eyes were blue, but washed out and faded like the sucked pulp of a muscadine and they never seemed to steady in one direction. His hands moved with them and in the same way, never fast but never still. When he finished eating he wiped his mouth on a napkin and leaned back in his chair.

"Court's in term," he said to Uncle Zack, "and I won't be able to holp you out."

Uncle Zack and Aunt Soph looked upset about that and Uncle Zack said, "Sheriff, there's always trouble when deliveries start."

Sheriff Foster said he knew it. "I figgered to deputize somebody to keep order," he said and looked at Big Eli. "As long as your brother is learning the tobacco business, it might as well be him."

"He could do it," Uncle Zack said, and then asked, "how about it, Elias?"

"I don't hanker," said Big Eli.

Sheriff Foster thought for a spell.

"If it wasn't for Zack there wouldn't be no village of Humility," he said. "That warehouse of his *is* Humility. Burn it down or take it away and folks would move away. It's his responsibility to keep order in a place he made."

Uncle Zack didn't say anything about that and the Sheriff went on telling Big Eli that it wouldn't be a regular job, but only while deliveries were being made.

"You'd oblige me to take it," he said.

"On one condition," said Big Eli.

"What's that?" said the Sheriff.

"I won't tote a gun," said Big Eli, and I knew the Sheriff would have to take it or leave it.

"That's up to you," said the Sheriff, "but there are low-down critters hereabouts. I'd advise you to tote one."

Big Eli shook his head. "No gun," he said.

The Sheriff reached into his pocket and brought out a bright badge and tossed it across the table to Big Eli.

"Then make certain you keep this in sight," he said, and got to his feet. "Stand up, Elias," he said and raised his right hand.

Big Eli got up and raised his right hand and the Sheriff recited the oath and Big Eli said, "I do."

"If anything happens you can't handle," said the Sheriff, "I can manage to come over from Wadesboro." He thanked Aunt Soph for his supper, shook hands around and left.

We went to bed in less than an hour after he left and soon after the clock on the mantel struck midnight I heard the first wagon groan down the road. I could tell by the cussing of the driver and the sound of the wheels in the mud that it was loaded heavy. Other wagons followed in the next two hours and I heard Uncle Zack get up and go to the kitchen and chunk the fire. Then he came in and woke Big Eli who was still snoring. Aunt Soph went to the kitchen to get breakfast. Big Eli roused the fire in the big room and got into his work riggin' and by that time I didn't want to go back to sleep, so I got up too.

I could see the glare of a bonfire flickering on the panes of the bay window and when I looked out I could see men standing around a blaze down near the warehouse. They were warming their hands and their rears. Uncle Zack came in the big room and went to the fireplace where he removed two bricks from the chimney. He brought out a bag of silver and the biggest roll of paper money I had ever seen, then he put the bricks back into place again. The clock struck three and we sat down to breakfast.

It was still black night when Uncle Zack and Big Eli started for the warehouse and I went with them. The men he had hired were waiting for him, two of them, and he opened the doors and Big Eli lit the turpentine lanterns that had been cleaned and filled the day before. Then the unloading and weighing started. Wagons would drive up and stop in front of the big double doors and the hired men took over, doing the unloading and handling the leaf while the farmer stood by the scales and tallied the weight and so did Uncle Zack. When a wagon was emptied and the weight figured, Uncle Zack would get out his money and pay up. The farmer would climb in the empty wagon, standing in the bed with his feet wide apart to balance himself, and drive off.

Most of them drove to the store to settle accounts that had been carried for months and some hung around the bonfires most of the day and told stories and drank grog before going home.

When the sun came up the thin snow began to melt but the wind was still raw and cold. Between twenty and thirty wagons were strung out along the road past the last house in the village. They were covered with blankets and quilts of many colors, tied down at the corners to keep them from blowing off and to keep the leaf from drying out in the wind. On top of the quilts, fence rails or heavy sticks of firewood had been laid to weight down the load so it wouldn't sway and topple if the wagon hit a bump in the road. When the wagons stopped in line the rails and sticks were used to keep the bonfires going, for there were two burning by daybreak. Now and then some of the men would go into the forest and bring more wood, mostly the dead limbs that had broken off under the weight of the passenger pigeons a long time before.

The road was deep with mud as the loaded wagons had cut deep ruts almost to the hubs and sometimes the mules had trouble in getting the load moving again once it had stopped and settled. When that happened men left the bonfires and waded to their boot tops in the mud to strain and pull at the rear wheels and get the wagon moving toward the warehouse. There were several yokes of oxen hitched to wagons and they never seemed to have any trouble getting their loads moving. Mules and horses plunged and sometimes fell when their loads wouldn't budge and had to be helped to their feet by men.

The oxen only lowered their shaggy heads and laid against the yoke while the drivers yelled oaths and cracked bull whips that sounded like pistol shots in the winter air. The wagons would creak and then slowly move while the mud made sucking sounds around the wheels and the legs of the oxen. Nobody bothered to help the oxen because they didn't need it. But the men who stood around the bonfires would yell advice to the bullwhackers and some of it was mighty smutty, but not as smutty as the oaths the bullwhackers yelled at the oxen.

Mule skinners liked to tell stories about bullwhackers and bullwhackers liked to tell stories about mule skinners and I guess they tried to undo each other.

"Ever hear the one about the bullwhacker who stopped at the farmer's house and asked to stay all night?" a mule skinner asked the men about the bonfire, and if anybody had heard it they didn't let on. So he told it.

The mule skinner doubled up laughing at his own joke and so did everybody else. They laughed so loud Aunt Soph came to the window to see if a fight had started. That night when we were eating supper I thought I'd make Uncle Zack and Big Eli laugh like that so I said, "Did you ever hear the story about the bullwhacker who stopped at a farmer's house and asked to stay all night?"

Uncle Zack nearly swallowed his fork and Big Eli leaned way back in his chair and laughed louder than the men had, only I hadn't told it.

Aunt Soph tried to smother a grin with her apron but before I could say a word she said, "I think they've heard it, Little Eli." Then she snapped, "And I don't want to hear it."

CHAPTER XIII

I SPENT most of my time around the bonfires listening to the stories and watching the mule skinners and bullwhackers play games to waste away the time until their wagons were unloaded. The games usually started after a jug had been passed around and sometimes they ended in fights and the men would roll in the mud and gouge at each other's throats and eyes and batter each other with their fists. Now and then Big Eli would have to come down from the warehouse and straighten things out. If they didn't stop by the time he got there, he'd reach down and grab them by the collars and jerk them standing. He'd warn them and go back to work. They didn't seem to mind his butting in for by the time he did both fighters were so tired they could hardly stand up anyway. A couple of times he had to take knives away from them but nobody crossed with him. I don't know whether it was because he was so big and strong or because of the bright badge on his coat. He never tried to stop the games which got mighty rough at times.

They had one game called "Howdy Stranger." Two men would stand sidewise and toe to toe, with their feet wide apart so they wouldn't get thrown off balance when the game started. Each man would put his left hand on his hip and it had to stay there during the game or the man who lifted his left hand would be called the loser. They would say "Howdy Stranger" and clasp hands and the game was on. Each one would try to crush the other's hand until he quit. They would sway back and forth and grunt and groan with pain until the sweat would roll down their faces and now and then I'd hear a bone break or a wrist crack and the hurt one would quit.

Another game was called "Rapjack" and it was played mostly by bullwhackers because they knew how to cut the wings off a horsefly with their bull whips which were fifteen to twenty feet long. Two of them would square off about fifteen feet apart and one would usually say, "No eyes," and the other would repeat, "No eyes," which meant it wouldn't be fair to aim at eyes during the game. Then they'd start lashing out with their whips, first picking off buttons which would go flying through the air, and then they would start ripping jeans. The whips would snap and crack like rifle shots and a knife couldn't cut cloth any keener. More than once I saw a man's rigging' stripped off him and he'd have to wrap up in a quilt like an Injun to keep warm. Now and then a bullwhacker would misjudge his aim and draw blood and the crowd would yell. The man whose blood had been drawn would then set out to draw some for himself. They would stand and cut at each other with the long whips until both would be stripped of hide and covered with blood and Big Eli would have to come from the warehouse and stop it. Doc Haney, who bled horses and was the coroner, had to sew up some of the bullwhackers after such fights.

It was the day after Big Eli stopped a whip fight that he had trouble with Stan Bodine. Bodine had come to Humility every day since deliveries started. Big Eli and I saw him drive up in a hack with a spatterboard and a high seat. The wheels were spoked with hickory painted red and the bed, which was black with red trimmings, set back from the seat about two feet. He had a fancy horsehair blanket covering his knees and another one covering something else in the bed of the hack.

He didn't hitch near the warehouse but tied up his horse near the tavern. Men around the bonfires grinned when they saw him and joked him when he joined them.

"You don't plow a furrow with them nags," one of them said, meaning the horses were too good for hard work.

"I didn't plow a furrow to get 'em, either," said Bodine and winked.

"Mighty cold day," said another farmer. "Takes more'n a fire to keep a body warm."

Bodine grinned but didn't say anything.

"Got anything beside burning chunks to keep a body warm, Stan?" another farmer asked.

"For a man who can pay for it, I have," he said.

"I might freeze before Zack Wakefield unloads my crop and pays up," said the farmer and waved a hand at the line of wagons waiting to be unloaded.

"I reckon your credit's good until then," Bodine said.

He turned and started toward his rig and the farmer followed him. Soon the farmer came back with a jug under his coat. He uncorked it, flipped it over his wrist and drank, then made a wry face and spit into the fire. Blue flame bounced up and flickered for more than a minute.

"Burns better than chunks," he said, and everybody laughed. He passed the jug and it went from man to man around the bonfire. When it was empty the farmer tossed the jug to the top of his load. Two more farmers went away with Bodine in the afternoon and came back with jugs and Bodine stood around the fire and joked with the men and collected the money he had been promised in the morning.

One afternoon a whip fight started and Big Eli came from the warehouse to stop it when it got bloody. Bodine saw him and the fun that had been in his face up to then seemed to drain into his boots and his fat lips sagged into a snarl.

"I'll be darned," he said, "look who's toting a badge on his chest."

That was the first the two whip fighters knew that Big Eli was on his way and when they saw him they quit lashing at each other and one of them went to his wagon and tossed his whip on the load. The other one pocketed his whip. Big Eli came up to the bonfire like he had just dropped by to talk. He looked at two jugs on the ground and then at Stan Bodine who looked him back square in the eye. Big Eli turned and went back to the warehouse.

The next day Bodine came back with another load of jugs and Big Eli and I were standing in the door of the warehouse when we saw his rig pull up at the tavern. He wasn't alone this time. Hannah was in the seat beside him, wrapped in a fancy horsehair blanket. Bodine climbed down out of the seat and helped her out and they went in the tavern together.

"It's her," I said and looked at Big Eli.

"I see," he said and went back to work.

Bodine came out of the tavern and drove his rig around to the hitch rack at the side. Then he came down the road and joined the farmers and bullwhackers at the bonfire. I stayed at the warehouse with Big Eli and Uncle Zack.

When we went to the house to eat at noon, Miss Susie Spann was helping Aunt Soph. She hadn't done this before and I wondered why she was helping now. Then I remembered she lived across the road from the tavern and I guessed she must have seen Hannah ride into the village with Bodine. Big Eli wasn't in a mind for talk. He minced his vittles and hardly looked at Miss Susie even when she drew a chair and sat beside him. He and Uncle Zack went back to the warehouse without waiting for the peach cobbler with cinnamon on top which Miss Susie said she had cooked herself. I couldn't pass it up and I didn't go with them.

When Big Eli and Uncle Zack left, Miss Susie helped clear the table and every time she would pass the kitchen window she would look up the road toward the tavern as if she expected Big Eli might sneak up to the tavern to see Hannah. Finally she said to Aunt Soph, "What is she like, Mrs. Wakefield?"

Aunt Soph looked at me and then at Miss Susie.

"Little pitchers have big ears," she said, and I knew she wanted Miss Susie to say nothing about Hannah where I could hear her. I got up from the table and went outside.

Two wagons were going up the road to turn at the tavern and swing into line with the others waiting to be unloaded. One was driven by Bob Morgan but he was too busy keeping his team moving to hear me when I yelled at him. The other wagon was drawn by four mules and it was swaying from side to side under the load. The driver was standing on the tongue and leaning back against the load and he was having all he could do to handle the reins. A boy about my own age was straddling the rear off critter and laying a short whip to the rumps of the lead span.

The wagon was sunk in the mud almost to the hubs and the mules were straining and plunging under their load. The men around the bonfire stopped talking and watched, for anything could have happened. I was afraid the tongue would be pulled out and I wouldn't have wanted to be that boy if it did, and yet I envied him for everybody was as concerned about him as I was. The team made the turn at last and came into line. Talk began around the bonfire.

Bob Morgan came down to the fire and spoke to the men and when he saw me he asked why Big Eli and I hadn't been to see him and his brothers and what we had been doing since we last saw them. The boy joined up with us and warmed his hands, which were red and swollen with the cold. The whip-stock was in his back pocket with the rawhide lash coiled loose around it, and I knew he had made it himself. It was like the whips the bullwhackers used only it was about four feet long instead of twenty. I looked up and saw him looking at my long hair as interested as I was in his whip. His face was thin but tanned brown as an Injun's, and he was shivering a little for he wasn't wearing a coat. Neither of us said anything but stood there looking at each other.

I was wondering if I had anything he would swap for the whip in his pocket when I heard Stan Bodine, who was standing next to him, say, "He just looks like a girl, so don't try to kiss him."

The men laughed and the boy pinked a little through his tan. Stan Bodine grinned and squinted his eyes like a pig wading through a briar patch. "Maybe he is a girl," he said to the boy.

The boy shifted his eyes to the crowd and away from me like he wished somebody would start talking about mules or something else.

I looked at Bob Morgan and saw he was getting mad.

"Let the boys alone, Bodine," he said. The men about the fire looked from Bob to Bodine for they expected trouble then. Bob had walked around the fire and I started with him but as I did, Bodine gave the boy a push which he wasn't looking for and he stumbled against me and fell to his knees. Just then a man pushed through the crowd. He was the one I had seen riding the wagon tongue and handling the reins on the four-mule team. He saw the boy on his knees beside me and his face, which was pinched and lined from sun and work, got tight as a goatskin over a pickle crock and his lips bleached white. The boy saw him and I knew he was scared as he got up from the ground and backed away from me. He never took his eyes off his father but he didn't say anything.

"Whip him, Son," the man said, "or I'll hide you!"

The boy reached for the whip in his back pocket and before I could dodge I felt it cut across my face and I lunged to get close to him so he couldn't hit me again. He was strong even if he was skinny and he broke away. Blood started running down my face and over my eyes. I saw a stick on the ground and grabbed it and swung at him and I heard him yell. Then I saw that the stick was ablaze. I had pulled it out of the fire. The whip cut me again, this time across the back, and I heard my jerkin split like it had been slashed with a knife, and again I swung the burning stick and the charred end broke over his head.

We stood there swinging at each other, but because my stick had broken he had the best of me and never missed with the whip and blood was running down my back and legs. I heard him crying and I began to cry too and all the time I could hear Stan Bodine egging us on but always backing the one who seemed to be beating the other. Then things got quiet all of a sudden and I felt a hand on my shoulder and it shoved me back and knocked the stick out of my hand. I wiped a hand across my eyes to clear away the blood and sweat and I saw the boy backing away, shaking like he had the palsy and looking at somebody back of me like he was scared half to death.

"I didn't want to fight! I didn't want to fight!" he kept saying as he backed away.

I turned and saw Big Eli and the deputy sheriff's badge on his shirt shining bright in the afternoon sun.

The boy's father pushed in and said, "He knocked my boy down!" Big Eli didn't pay him any heed, but he asked the boy, "Did he start this?" and the boy shook his head and said, "They made us fight."

"Who made you fight?" asked Big Eli, and the boy looked around at the crowd as if he was blaming everybody instead of Stan Bodine. Big Eli looked at Bob Morgan but didn't say anything.

"Bodine egged 'em into it," Bob said.

Big Eli faced Bodine who was leaning against the muddy wheel of a tobacco wagon.

"Bodine, I'm arresting you," said Big Eli.

That was the first time I had heard him say that he would arrest anybody. He had only stopped fights before and then gone back to his work in the warehouse.

"For what?" Bodine snarled and the grin was gone from his face.

"Disturbing the peace," said Big Eli and started toward him.

Stan Bodine shifted his eyes to the men about the fire but he didn't get a friendly look back and then I saw him reach out and snatch a bull whip which was on the seat of the wagon he had been leaning against. He gave the stock a quick little flip and by the way the lash coiled in his fingers I knew he had used a bull whip before and plenty. Right then I wished that Big Eli had taken the Sheriff's advice and toted a gun.

Bodine stepped free of the wagon and braced himself on spread legs as Big Eli came at him and then, like he was popping the head off a snake, he flipped the whip and I saw the bright badge on Big Eli's chest go flying through the air. Bodine laughed and so did some of the others. As the whip cracked again, Big Eli covered his face with his left hand to protect his eyes but blood shot from his fingers and I saw a red welt cross his forehead. He tried to rush Bodine but the whip cracked and never missed. He was half blinded but he kept trying to get at Bodine who moved fast for his size and weight, keeping a distance of fifteen feet or more betwix them. Each time the long whip curled out it cracked like a rifle, and the crowd around the fire began to grow and women began looking out of doorways along the road.

Miss Susie Spann was watching from the door of our house and Aunt Soph was standing behind her wringing her hands.

I don't know how long the fight had been going on, but it seemed hours to me, and Big Eli hadn't laid a hand on Bodine. His shirt had been ripped to shreds and his big shoulders and neck were cut and bleeding and so was his face and arms. The grin had disappeared from Bodine's face and sweat was running down the fat furrows which he didn't bother to wipe away.

The tip of the lash stripped a yard of cloth from Big Eli's jeans and one leg was laid bare, and again Bodine's whip cracked and the other pants leg ripped and rolled to the ground to be dragged through the mud as Big Eli moved about, trying to get away from the whip. I couldn't stand it any longer, for I was crying mad, and I reached down and picked up a burning chunk from the fire. Before I had a chance to throw it at Bodine, Bob Morgan knocked it from my hand.

"Keep out of this or you'll get hurt," he said.

Big Eli must have seen it happen for he rushed Bodine fast and Bodine had to sidestep to get out of his way. As Bodine did he had his back to Morgan and me and I saw him raise his right hand above his shoulders to bring down the lash on Big Eli again. It curled like a striking adder over my head and I saw a hand reach out and grab it. Bodine swung the stock forward but it jerked from his hand and sailed high in the air like Big Eli's badge had done.

He and I turned at the same time to see who had done it, and it was Bob Morgan. Bob coiled the whip in his fingers, ready to strike and Bodine halted.

"I'll get you for that," Bodine yelled, but he didn't try then for he saw Big Eli.

It wasn't exactly a cheer that ran through the crowd but was more like a sudden stir of wings when a flock of swallows take flight from a leafy tree. Bodine braced himself and put up his fists, but he didn't push the fight and he glanced sideways to see if he could get away. Big Eli had him cornered. He didn't slug him as I thought he would but his big fists slashed at the fat face like the whip had done to him and each time he did blood oozed from Bodine's face and ran down his neck.

Big Eli was backing him toward the loaded wagon and Bodine was covering with his arms and hands and kicking out now and then at Big Eli. And then he fell sprawling in the mud. Big Eli jerked him to his feet and slashed at him until he fell again. Bodine was as bloody as Big Eli but the mud was caked over him, red and like a paste.

Once Big Eli stopped and laughed at him, and the men about the fire laughed too. Bodine tried to run and Big Eli didn't try to stop him. Bodine fell to his knees and mired in the mud like a fat hog, and then Big Eli dragged him to his feet and, like he was taking aim at a buck a mile away, drew back his fist and drove it into Bodine's face and blood and mud spattered in all directions. Bodine sagged down into the road and rolled over like he was dead. Big Eli stood over him, wiping his hands on what was left of his jeans, and then he turned to Bob Morgan.

"His rig's at the tavern," he said. "Go get it."

Bob Morgan pushed through the crowd, and Big Eli said to me, "Go get her," and I knew he meant Hannah.

She was waiting in the door of the tavern as I came up to her and I didn't know what to say except, "Something's happened. You'd better come." I walked beside her and when the men in the crowd saw us coming they opened a path for us. She stopped in front of Big Eli and looked at him, saw the cuts and blood and his torn rags, and then she looked at Stan Bodine.

"Is he dead?" she asked Big Eli.

Big Eli looked her square like she was a stranger to him.

"No, but the only reason he ain't is because he's yours," he said.

Bob Morgan drove up in the rig. Big Eli lifted Bodine to his shoulder and when the crowd made way Hannah went ahead of him and he swayed through the mud after her. He rolled Stan Bodine into the seat and she climbed up beside him and took the reins. I saw her look over and back of me and I turned. There was Miss Susie Spann taking it all in and there was a faint smile on her lips and a light in her eyes I didn't like. Hannah slapped the reins and the two horses moved off toward the timber and the lane that led through it.

Doc Haney was standing next to Miss Susie and his kit was in his hand. I guessed somebody had gone for him. Big Eli saw him.

"Come, Doc," he said. "I'll need some stitches."

When we got in the house, the wagons had started to move again. Big Eli told Doc to look me over first, but I wasn't hurt bad and Aunt Soph and Miss Susie took me to the kitchen and washed off the blood and mud.

Big Eli told me to go outside. He didn't want me to see him being sewed up.

The bonfire had about burned out and I chunked it. Then I looked for Big Eli's badge but couldn't find it. The wagon with four mules strained and groaned through the mud toward me. Astride the rear off critter was the boy I had the fight with and his face was still smeared with the charr from the burned stick I had whacked him with. When he saw me he grinned and I grinned back but we didn't say anything. As he passed he looked at the whip he held in his hand like he was trying to make up his mind about something. Then he let it drop to the ground. I waited to see if it was an accident that he dropped it but when he looked back and grinned I knew he meant for me to have it and I picked it up, but when he was out of sight I stuck it under the coals and in a few seconds bright yellow flames jumped up and then turned to blue. That's the way rawhide burns. I didn't want that whip any more.

CHAPTER XIV

When Uncle Zack was through receiving the crop he began sorting the leaf into grades and he spent a lot of time teaching Big Eli how it was done. The longest and widest leaves were the best if they were heavy and smooth and hadn't been damaged by worms. These were put into piles by themselves. Damaged leaves and short ones, which were generally lighter in color, were sorted into another pile and called lugs. The different grades were then made up into bales or stored in hogsheads for curing and then they were ready for shipment to New Orleans. The bales and hogsheads were hauled by wagon to the Tennessee where they were put aboard keelboats and Kentucky broadhorns. Only the keelboats went all the way to New Orleans. The broadhorns went down river to Pekin, where the Tennessee joined the Ohio, and their loads were then shifted to keelboats which made the trip west on the Ohio to the Mississippi and south to New Orleans.

When a load had to be shifted from broadhorn to keelboat, Uncle Zack and Big Eli went along with the shipment to Pekin.

"Them broadhorn men have a habit of forgetting to put all the load aboard the keels," Uncle Zack said. "I have to watch 'em like a hawk."

I had heard a lot about the men who ran the broadhorns, how they feared nobody and claimed to be the toughest men on the river. I got to know how tough they were while the shipping season was on. They liked to fight just for the fun of it and when they couldn't pick a fight they'd maul each other about. They had a song about how tough they were.

> My mammy was a gaiter,
> My pappy was a bull,
> I can whip my weight in wildcats
> And drink my belly full.

They were noisy men and they laughed and yelled a lot but they worked hard and were not afraid of the river. I saw them load a broadhorn until the ramp was less than a foot out of water and then pole out into the current to race some keelboater coming downstream from the shoals.

I went with Uncle Zack and Big Eli on one of the trips to Pekin. We were almost in sight of the Ohio when I saw a bunch of flatboats standing off a sandbar about a hundred yards. I had never seen flatboats like them before. They had racks on each side and lines hung down from the racks into the water. When the broadhorn men saw them, one yelled, "Mussel fleet!" and grabbed up his long pole and jumped into the prow of the broadhorn. The other broadhorn men picked up their poles and shoved them into the water and began pushing with all their might. The broadhorn swung toward the flatboats. The flatboaters started pulling up their drag anchors and rowing toward the sandbar as fast as they could, but some of them were too slow.

"Dive, blast you, dive!" the broadhorn men yelled as they bore down, and they held out their long poles just above the water. There was a crash and splintering of wood as the long poles hit the racks of the flatboats, and cuss words filled the air. The flatboaters tried to jump over the poles but some of them were knocked into the river. The broadhorn men yelled and laughed.

"Dive, you polecats, dive!" they whooped.

One flatboater made no move to get out of the way of the broadhorn. He stood up in his boat with a long rifle cupped under his arm and pointed at us. The broadhorn men poled back into the current and left him alone.

"What're they fishing for?" I asked Uncle Zack when we passed below the flatboaters.

"Mussels," he said. "They sell the shells to make pearl buttons out'n."

Late that day the mussel fishermen came ashore at Pekin and unloaded their catch and Big Eli and Uncle Zack and I watched them. Soon a man, driving a light wagon, came down and began buying the shells by the bushel. I could see that

Uncle Zack was surprised at the prices the man was paying and he asked the buyer a lot of questions. On the way up river the next day we passed a bunch of flatboaters hovering over a mussel bed but the broadhorn men were too busy poling against the current to bother them.

"I was thinking," said Uncle Zack to Big Eli, "that when work slacks off you might give that a try." He motioned toward the mussel fishermen. "You can make day wages or better," he said.

I might have known why Uncle Zack was asking questions of the shell buyer. He never showed interest in anything unless there was money in it. About a month after we had been to Pekin, Big Eli started building a flatboat. He let me help tar the seams and when that was done we racked the boat on sawhorses and let it set and season. He was building the racks for the drag lines when the spring rains, which were late, started in and they didn't let up for a week.

The big river went out of its banks and spread through the bottoms. Some people had to move out and we heard that a couple of families didn't make it in time and were drowned. One night, Anse Morgan came up from his bottom farm in a wagon. He had seen Big Eli working on the flatboat and had tried to draw him out as to what Big Eli was going to do with it. When he pulled up at Uncle Zack's, he said to Big Eli, "I don't know what you built that boat for, but it would come in right handy to me and my brothers right now."

"How so?" Big Eli asked.

"Much of our land in under water," Anse said, "and some of our stock is marooned on high ground. If the river gets higher they'll drown. With that boat we can get 'em out."

"Then she's yours," said Big Eli.

"Ever handle a boat in a flood?" Anse asked. "It's risky business."

"It'll take more than a flood to upset this one," Big Eli said. "I can handle it."

Anse climbed out of his wagon and he and Big Eli lifted the flatboat into the bed. Big Eli went to tell Aunt Soph and Uncle Zack where we were going while I went to the warehouse and got the oars which we had finished that day. We drove in the rain to Anse Morgan's place where we spent the night, and by daybreak the rain had slackened to a cold drizzle. His brothers came in while we were eating breakfast and then we went outside to look at the flooded bottoms. The river was almost two miles wide in places and on either side of the main current, only islands showed above water.

"If the rain don't let up, most of them will be under in twenty-four hours," Tully Morgan said.

The roof of a barn floated downstream and snags of trees bobbed up and down and rolled over and over in the current. The boat was unloaded from the wagon and slid into the water which had backed up almost to Anse Morgan's barn and stables. Big Eli handled the oars and the Morgan brothers worked in shifts with him. Two of them went out on each trip and they prowled between the islands until they saw stock and then they'd push ashore and tie up. It was easy enough to herd the hogs aboard the flatboat. They seemed to know they were being helped from certain death and they huddled together and gave Big Eli and the Morgans no trouble. But cows were different. They had to be thrown and tied to keep them in the boat until they could be landed on high ground. Two mules and a horse were roped and led into the water to swim behind the flatboat when Big Eli shoved off, and when they got to Anse Morgan's place they clambered out of the water and shook themselves.

Big Eli and the Morgans worked for two days saving stock and a lot of it wasn't theirs but belonged to other bottom farmers who claimed them later on. The rains stopped meanwhile but the river was still rising and only tree tops could be seen on some of the islands we had sighted that first morning.

"What's the tally now?" Big Eli asked.

"We've got most of 'em," said Tully, and his brothers agreed.

"There's a cow and a calf missing," said Anse, "but unless we sight her from here there's no sense looking now."

"We'll look in the morning," said Big Eli.

That night I asked Big Eli if I could go along because he hadn't taken me in the boat once. He seemed against it, but I begged hard.

"I'll stay in the prow and not get in the way," I promised, and he finally nodded his head and said, "All right, Little Eli, I reckon it'll be safe enough."

The sun rose bright the next morning and when we shoved into the water I was in the prow and Big Eli was at the oars, his big broad back toward me. Bob and Tully Morgan were in the stern. Anse had sighted the cow on one of the small islands and he stood on high ground waving directions to Big Eli, and it wasn't long until the boat nosed ashore. Bob and Tully went after the cow and calf. Soon I saw them coming back. Bob was toting the calf in his arms and Tully was herding the cow ahead of him. Bob laid the calf in the flatboat and helped Tully get the cow aboard. They tied her legs but didn't throw her as they figgered she wouldn't get rambunctious because of her calf. Her weight settled the boat deep into the mud and Bob and Tully had to pole us into deep water again. Big Eli was having plenty to do to keep the boat headed against the current, and because his back was toward the prow he didn't see what I was watching.

Many trees had been uprooted by the flood and were floating downstream, mostly in the main current. One, green with leaves, had been caught by an eddy and was drifting in quiet water but it kept swinging around and around. Two crows were wheeling above it and making an awful clatter about something. Now and then they would dive into the branches and out again to chatter and scream. I knew that somewhere in the tree was a nest of young crows.

The roots of the tree dragged bottom and it looked like the tree might settle down and stay there. Big Eli was swaying at the oars and the Morgan brothers were poling with all their might. I was the only one who saw what happened. As the boat came abreast of the roots, a swell in the current lifted the branchy end of the tree and it swung toward us. I let out a yell and Big Eli turned his head and saw it. He jerked an oar to turn the boat into the clear, but it was too late. I raised my hands to protect my eyes from the branches as the tree rolled over and the next second we were being lashed by the whirling limbs.

I clawed them away from me and I felt the boat sag under the weight as the top of the tree rolled over us, but it was all over. Bob Morgan had lost his hat and Big Eli's shirt was ripped almost off him. The boat had turned half around and Big Eli was trying to keep it steady until the Morgans could pole it to a stop and when they did Big Eli turned to look at me. I guess I was shaking, I was so scared and I knew it had all been my fault. I had been so took up with the two crows that I didn't yell a warning in time. Big Eli laughed.

"What've you got there?" he asked, and for the first time I realized I had something in my hand.

I looked down and saw I was holding what had been a crow's nest and I felt something flutter and saw it was a baby crow, still white with down.

I heard the two old crows screaming below us. They were wheeling above the tree which was turning over and over, and then it hit deep water and sank but the crows went on circling and screaming over where it disappeared. The Morgan brothers got the boat on keel and Big Eli bent at the oars.

I opened the front of my shirt and put the baby crow in next to my hide where it would be warm. It snuggled down and was quiet. Before Big Eli pushed ashore at Anse Morgan's place, I had thought up a name for the crow. I got it from Scripture. Moses.

CHAPTER XV

"RIVER MEN are riffraff," Miss Susie told Aunt Soph, "and shell fishermen are the lowest of the lot."

"I'll talk to Zachariah about it," Aunt Soph promised.

That night Aunt Soph did speak to Uncle Zack about it when Big Eli was at the stables feeding the stock.

"I've got to keep him busy to make him earn his keep," Uncle Zack said, "and while I'm doing it I might as well make a little profit too."

Aunt Soph didn't understand and Uncle Zack told her that button companies were paying well for mussel shells.

"I'll sell them to companies in Cincinnati," he told her.

"That's different," Aunt Soph said, "but it's not genteel work for your brother."

"He won't be doing it long," said Uncle Zack. "If Elias finds a bed worth working, I'll hire some fishermen. If he don't, it'll be his time and not my money that's been wasted."

The next day I told Big Eli what Uncle Zack had said and he laughed. "I'm on to Zack," he said.

"Then why are you going to do it?" I asked.

"There are some things I want to think over," he told me, "and the big river is a good place to sit and think."

I had felt that Big Eli didn't like working for Uncle Zack and for a while I wasn't certain he liked work at all, but when I saw him do the work of three men during the tobacco season I knew I was wrong about that. Now I wondered what it was he had to think about. Was it Miss Susie? Was it Hannah? Or was it me? I'd wait and find out.

The river was down again and running at medium stage when we put the boat in the river and put up the racks on each side. Big Eli bought a charcoal burner and an iron pot which he set up in the stern of the boat. We attached small weights to the lines and Big Eli rowed about a mile upstream and then we lowered the racks so the lines would drag bottom when we passed over a sandbar.

"Now we'll drift back," Big Eli said.

The current was not fast like it had been at flood, but Big Eli had to keep moving the oars against it to hold the boat at a slow pace. We kept near the east bank for most of the sandbars were on that side of the river. Twice before noon we made the trip up the river and drifted back down again without striking a mussel bed, and Big Eli slid the stone anchor over the side and brought the boat to a standstill.

"Let's take a dive before we eat," he said and began shuckin' his clothes, and I did too. In no time we were both splashing around in the water. The surface was warm but under the current was cool. We didn't put on our riggin' when we climbed back into the boat to eat the snack we had brought along. We let the sun dry us off first.

Late in the afternoon we struck a small bed of mussels and I pulled up the racks. There were more than a dozen shells clamped to the weights and the ends of the lines but instead of starting a charcoal fire under the pot and boiling them loose, Big Eli took his knife and pried them open.

"There's a trick to it," he said, and showed me how, by cutting through the hinge of the two shells, it killed the mussel and the shell popped open. The outside was rough and greenish but, when the meat was scraped out, the inside was slick and glossy like the butt of a dueling pistol.

Big Eli pointed to the gloss. "That's what they make buttons out'n," he said.

Just before sundown we tied up the boat and headed for Humility, taking a few of the shells with us for Uncle Zack to see. He thought they were good quality and told Big Eli to keep looking for a bed that would pay off. I didn't care whether we did or not. We were having fun, Big Eli and me, just drifting up and down the river. Sometimes we'd sing but most of the time we just lolled in the bright sun or took a dive, and now and then Big Eli would seem to forget where he was or that I was with him and I'd catch him looking off into space or into the water. He was thinking things over, but what I didn't know.

We made the first good strike on the third day and dropped the anchor in about ten feet of water. The lines were loaded when we lifted the racks and Big Eli started the charcoal fire and soon had the pot of water boiling. Then he picked up the lines and dropped them into the hot water and the mussels popped open and let go the weights. Big Eli fished out the shells and dropped them into the bottom of the boat after he scraped out the meat and tossed it into the river where big buffalo fish surfaced and gobbled it up. During the rest of the day Big Eli would let out the anchor line slow so the weights from the racks would drag over the mussel bed ten feet below us. When the boat reached the end of the anchor line he would play it back until we reached the an-chor again. After the first day of our strike, it was my job to lift the racks and drop the shells into the boiling water while Big Eli played the boat over the mussel bed.

The flies were bad because the mussels had a fishy smell that was higher than a sick carp and it got on our hands and riggin'. After a few days soap and water couldn't get shed of it.

The first night after we made the strike we saw Faro come running to meet us as we got near Uncle Zack's house in Humility, but when we got within a few yards of him he stopped dead in his tracks like he had made a mistake and didn't know us. He started to growl and the bristles raised on his neck and it wasn't until Big Eli spoke to him and laughed that he knew for certain it was us. I almost had a fight with some boys the next night when they called me "stink fish" as I walked past.

Uncle Zack was always the first to leave for meeting on Sunday morning. He opened the doors of his warehouse and put up the benches for folks to sit on and then he stood by the door and shook hands with folks as they came in. The Sunday after we found the mussel bed, Big Eli and I waited until Aunt Soph had cleared the breakfast dishes and then we heated water and got ready to scrub down with lye soap. Aunt Soph went on ahead of us to meeting. When we got there she was sitting beside Miss Susie and there were two spaces left for us because folks had learned we all sat together. I let Big Eli slide in on the bench next to Miss Susie and then I sat beside him. We had been sitting there a couple of minutes when I saw the tavern keeper's wife turn around and look at us and then hold her kerchief over her nose. She whispered to the blacksmith's wife, who was sitting next to her, and she began holding her nose too.

Somebody back of us sniggered and then I looked around and folks were holding their noses or covering them with kerchiefs. Just before Uncle Zack mounted the hogshead to lead singing and start preaching, Miss Susie Spann got up out of her seat.

"Excuse me," she said.

Big Eli stood up to let her pass. She put her kerchief over her nose and went across the aisle to sit with her brother.

Uncle Zack had to pound his fists to quiet things down so he could start the meeting. I knew then it would take more than lye soap to get the stink off of us.

That afternoon I heard Aunt Soph talking to Uncle Zack about it. "We're the laughingstock of the village," she said.

Aunt Soph never did anything she thought would make folks displeased with her and it upset her a heap when Big Eli and I did.

CHAPTER XVI

FOLKS called Zybee Fletcher the snake doctor. He didn't doctor snakes but traveled from place to place peddling herb cures. He carried his wares in a heavy case which he would set up on a pair of crisscrossed iron standards when he got in a village such as Humility. Beside his herb cures, Zybee also carried a lot of bottles with snakes inside, pickled in alcohol. He would put these in plain sight where everybody could see them and it always drew a crowd. Two of them were rattlers and big ones. One had fourteen buttons on its tail and the other had eight. In another bottle was a snake he called a cobra and its neck was spread out flat like a fried egg. When the crowd got big enough Zybee would spend the first half hour telling big tales about the snakes and how he came by them.

"This rattler here," he'd say and pick up the bottle with the fourteen-button snake, "killed fifty men before it was captured in the fever infested swamps of Florida." The other one, he claimed, had attacked him in California but he had captured it alive by a charm he had learned from a Hindu in India.

Then he'd show the cobra and say it was the favorite snake of the Hindu who had taught him the charm. But he saved his big speech for a little snake no bigger than a garter and which he said was an asp.

"The most venomous reptile known to man," he would shout, holding the bottle and turning it slow so everybody could see it. "This little snake, my friends, changed the course of civilization," he would say.

He would then wait for his words to sink in.

"A few years ago, while traveling in old Egypt," he would begin like a backsliding preacher, "I was approached one night by a leper whose sores oozed pus and so covered his body that he was hardly to be recognized as a human being. At first I was horrified that he should get so near me, but when he spoke I realized he was a member of the high caste, a man of great culture. So I listened to what he had to say. Into my ears he poured forth one of the great secrets of the world, a secret that had laid buried for hundreds of years. Then he led me to a tomb, musty with the weight of the ages, and from a vat of scented oil, he brought forth this venomous reptile then dead two thousand years."

Zybee Fletcher would pause at this point and study the bottle he held in his hand and everybody would crane their necks to get a better look at it. Then he'd start off again.

"No sooner had the leperous hands lifted the snake into mine than the old man fell dead at my feet, and I hurried from that ancient tomb in possession of a reptile that had done more to change the course of history than Hannibal, Alexander or Andy Jackson!"

By that time everybody was crowding closer to hear how the little snake did it. Zybee Fletcher would lower his voice like a turtle dove and tell about Mark Antony and Cleopatra. When he got to the part where Cleopatra killed herself, he would clutch at his shirt and yank it open and as he talked he shoved the bottle with the asp inside it.

"In her grief," he'd moan and shut his eyes, "that proud Queen of Old Egypt clutched to her boosom . . . this very asp I now hold in my hand. Once! Twice! Thrice! this venomous viper bit the royal boosom and before the poisonous fangs could strike again, the Queen was dead!"

Zybee would open his eyes and pull the bottle out of his shirt. Then he'd start selling his herb cures.

I first saw Zybee when Big Eli and I came to Humility to live with Uncle Zack. It was right after Hannah had run away when Old Decker and the Constable from Cadiz came to get her. The next time I saw him he was standing on the east bank of the Tennessee River late one afternoon. He was calling to Big Eli and me to come and get him and his herb case.

About a week before I had found something bright and shiny in one of the mussel shells and showed it to Big Eli. He held it in his fingers and eyed it a spell and then he said, "Little Eli, you've found a pearl."

"Pearls are worth lots of money," I said, remembering what I had learned from scriptures.

"Some are," he said.

"Is this one?" I asked.

"I don't know," he said, "but until we find out don't say anything to Uncle Zack about finding it."

"I won't," I said.

After that I looked into all of the shells and in the next few days I found a lot of pearls, some bigger than the first I had found and the rest not so big. None of them was as big as a pea and instead of being round, like I thought a pearl would be, they were all sorts of shapes but they were mighty pretty just the same. Big Eli kept them in his poke and now and then he'd take them out and hold them in the palm of his hand and let the sun shine on them.

When Zybee Fletcher hailed us to ferry him across the river, it was about time we knocked off for the day anyway. We hauled in the lines and I emptied the boiling pot into the river and threw out the burning charcoal. It spit and sizzled like a tomcat when it hit the water. Then Big Eli headed the boat toward Zybee.

He was wearing a tall beaver and a crow-tailed coat and he had his pants legs tucked in his boot tops to keep them from getting dusty. A heavy gold watch chain swung across his vest which was made of antelope tails. His boots were scuffed up plenty and I knew he had been walking a long way. When Big Eli nosed the boat into the river bank, Zybee greeted us like we were kin.

"Howdy, cousins," he said and tossed his case in the boat and climbed in. Then he saw the racks and lines.

"What's them?" he asked. Big Eli told him but he didn't waste any words. He started to shove off but Zybee stopped him.

"The least I can do is pull my own load," he said.

"Can you handle a boat?" Big Eli asked him.

Zybee threw back his head and laughed so loud it got crows ashore excited.

"Cousin," he said, "I was once a gondolier in the service of the Doges of Venice!"

Big Eli slid back to the prow and Zybee took the oars. He knew how to handle them all right and as he headed across the river he opened his big mouth and began to sing in words I didn't understand and the hills echoed his voice back to us. When he finished the first stanza he looked at me and grinned. *Song of the Gondoliers*, he said. It sounded like a yodel to me.

The mussel shells were still clamped to the lines and while he went on yodeling again, I took out my pocket-knife and began clipping the shells open. The third one I opened had a pearl in it. A big one. I held it up for Big Eli to see. Zybee Fletcher quit singing.

"Let's see that, Cousin," he said, and I showed it to him, wondering later if I had made a mistake. He laughed big.

"So that's what you're doing, Cousins," he said. "Searching for the wealth of kings!"

Big Eli started to explain we were fishing for mussel shells to sell to button makers, but Zybee Fletcher only laughed.

"You can't fool me, Cousin," he said. "You're hunting for pearls!"

"Is it worth anything?" I asked him, because I knew Zybee had been about and might know if it was.

Zybee kept on rowing. "To those who treasure pearls, it is priceless," he said. "Not me, I hanker diamonds."

He had plenty of diamonds on his fingers and in his bright blue cravat.

After we got across the river and tied up for the night, Zybee Fletcher asked me how many pearls we had found, but I didn't answer and looked at Big Eli instead.

"Or won't you tell me?" Zybee asked with a grin like he thought we were trying to hide something from him.

"We've found a few," said Big Eli. "We've been wondering if they're worth anything."

Zybee asked to see them and Big Eli got out his poke and

poured the pearls into the palm of his hand. The setting sun played rainbows on them.

Zybee cleared his throat. "Have you tried to sell them, Cousin?" he asked, and Big Eli said he hadn't.

"Then I'll share a secret, Cousin," he said and stuck his thumbs in the pockets of his vest. "I've just got back from a tour of Europe," he said. "While in old England I was a guest of His Majesty, George the Fourth. He confided to me that he is searching the world for pearls and he asked me to be on the lookout for pearls of good quality."

My ears started to hum and I looked at Big Eli and saw he was drinking it in too. "How about these?" Big Eli asked.

"Perfect specimen of fresh water pearls," said Zybee.

"How would I go about selling them to a king?" Big Eli asked him.

"A king is human, like the rest of us," said Zybee. "Just write him a letter and tell him how many you have, how big they are and where you got them. Be certain to tell him that, where you got them."

Big Eli nodded his head.

"And don't forget to mention my name," said Zybee. "It will carry its weight."

"I'll tell him," said Big Eli.

"You'd better not tell anybody I have shared this royal secret with you," Zybee said, looking around like somebody might be hiding in the bushes.

"I'll not," said Big Eli, "and don't you tell anybody I'm writing the letter."

"I won't, Cousin," said Zybee.

We started up the road to Humility and I wondered what Aunt Soph and Uncle Zack and Miss Susie would give to know that we were going to write a letter to a king.

CHAPTER XVII

WE DIDN'T go back to the river the next day. The post rider, who came to Humility twice a week, was due in with the mail. After breakfast Big Eli went to Uncle Zack's warehouse and I stayed in the back yard to play with Moses, the crow. By then he was jet black and half grown and hungry most of the time. He spent most of his time at the back door squalling for vittles, and Aunt Soph didn't like him because he made so much noise. Faro didn't like him either and would show his teeth and growl. Faro was jealous.

I had heard that crows could talk and I spent a lot of time that morning trying to teach Moses to say his name but he didn't seem to catch on. Uncle Zack heard me trying to teach Moses his name.

"You have to split a crow's tongue to make him talk," Uncle Zack said.

I had heard that before and asked Big Eli about it.

"No you don't," I said to Uncle Zack. "Big Eli says it's not true."

Uncle Zack shuffled his shoulders and went on about his business but I knew he still believed what he said because lots of people believed like he did.

I got a biscuit for Moses and when he finally filled his crop he flew to the tip top of the big maple in the back yard. I started to the warehouse to see what Big Eli was doing, but I met him halfway and he had a letter in his hand.

"I wrote it," he said, showing it to me.

I fell in step with him. "Are you going to post it?" I asked.

"Yes, the post rider just came in," he said, and I looked toward the tavern and saw the post rider's horse with the saddlebags swinging over his rump.

"Don't say anything to Uncle Zack or anybody about it," Big Eli told me and I said I wouldn't.

When we got to the tavern a lot of people were there and the post rider was calling out names and passing out mail he had brought. I took Uncle Zack's newspaper which he got once a week from St. Louis and also a letter for Aunt Soph from her sister in Carolina. After the mail was passed out, Big Eli went to the desk and handed the post rider the letter to the King. The post rider didn't seem to notice who it was being sent to, but when he put it on the scales to weigh it I saw him reading the name and where it was going. He looked up at Big Eli and studied him a second but he didn't say anything. The tavern keeper saw him looking at Big Eli and he took a look at the letter and then he and the post rider looked at each other. The post rider told Big Eli how much it would cost to send it and Big Eli paid him.

As we came out of the tavern, Zybee Fletcher was setting up his herb case and getting ready to sell his cures to the people when they came out. He smiled at us.

"Good morning, Cousins," he said.

Big Eli said howdy and paused for a minute. "I just sent the letter," he told the snake doctor.

Zybee looked surprised but he said, "Bravo, Cousin. You may soon be sleeping amid the wealth of the Empire."

In my mind's eye I saw Big Eli and me laying on a bed tick stuffed with golden feathers.

When I gave Uncle Zack his newspaper and Aunt Soph her letter I went back to hear Zybee Fletcher peddle his herb cures and tell stories about his pickled snakes. He wasn't in sight when I came out of the house and halfway to the tavern I passed the post rider and he grinned down from his horse and rode on. Zybee's herb case and bottled snakes were standing ready for him to go to work and I wondered where he had gone, and then I heard loud laughing in the tavern. I looked through the window and saw Zybee surrounded by the men who had been waiting for the mail. He was telling them something they thought was mighty funny. I moved close to the door and listened.

"So I told him the King was in the market for pearls and he'd better write the King a letter," Zybee was saying.

The crowd laughed and there was a lot of back slapping. Zybee was laughing so hard he could hardly go on with his talk, but I heard him say, "Them pearls ain't worth the picking," and he doubled up and slapped his knees, "but the big oaf took it hook, line and sinker."

I knew what he was talking about. He had made a fool of Big Eli on purpose and maybe he didn't even know the King of England as he had told us he did. Mussel pearls were no good after all and I knew we wouldn't be sleeping on a bed tick of golden feathers ever. I felt the blood running hot in my face and tears squeezing out the corners of my eyes. I turned away from the tavern door for I didn't want any of the men to see me, and at first I thought of running to Big Eli and telling him what I had heard, but I changed my mind.

I didn't want Big Eli to feel as bad as I was feeling and too I was afraid of what he might do to Zybee Fletcher. I had no hankering then to hear Zybee peddle his cures so I went back to Uncle Zack's, but I didn't go in the house and when Aunt Soph called me in at noon to eat I had lost my appetite complete.

"What's ailing you?" Big Eli asked me when I didn't touch the vittles on my plate.

"Nothing," I said and it was all I could do to keep from crying.

He looked at me with his soft blue eyes but he didn't say anything.

"Molasses and sulphur will cure what ails him," Aunt Soph said.

Big Eli shook his head. "Don't think so," he said. "It's not his belly that's ailing him, I'm thinking."

When he finished eating he got up from the table and went into the big room and got his rifle. "Want to go squirrel hunting, Little Eli?" he asked.

I did want to go but I was afraid to. I was afraid I'd tell him all about it when we were alone in the woods.

"I don't feel good," I said. He patted me on the back and walked out the door with the rifle and I heard Faro bark at the sight of the gun and go bounding off through the woods.

In the middle of the afternoon Zybee Fletcher packed his herb case and left with a chicken peddler, who had a wagon, for Paris. I was glad he did because I knew Big Eli would find out about it sooner or later and there was no telling what he would have done to the snake doctor for making a fool of him.

Uncle Zack came out of the house and sauntered up the road toward the tavern. A few minutes later I saw Miss Susie Spann coming toward me and she was in a big hurry. She barely spoke and disappeared in our door and I wondered what was up and started to follow her in. She saw me and said, "You play outside for a while, Little Eli." She closed the door.

About ten minutes later I saw Uncle Zack coming home and he was making tracks like a bobcat was after him.

"Has Elias come back yet?" he shouted at me and I said he hadn't, and he went in the house and shut the door. I knew he had found out.

About that time I heard Faro bark and saw him and Big Eli coming out of the woods and Big Eli had a bunch of squirrels slung over his shoulder. I didn't know what to do or say, but as he came up to me I said, "You'd better not go in now."

He looked at me, puzzled. "Why not?" he asked.

All I could think of to say was "Miss Susie and Uncle Zack are in there."

Big Eli tossed back his head and laughed.

"It's about the pearls," I said, knowing I couldn't hide it any longer. "They've found out, I think."

His face sobered and I saw him glance up the road toward the tavern. "Come on," he said, and we walked into the house, leaving the front door wide open again.

Uncle Zack and Aunt Soph and Miss Susie were sitting around the kitchen table when we walked through the big room and their faces were set as firm as an angel's on a tomb rock and just as solemn.

"Elias," said Uncle Zack, "why didn't you tell me about finding them pearls?"

Big Eli tossed the squirrels on the cook table and stacked the rifle against the door jam. "Because it wasn't none of your business, Zack," he said.

"Who got you started shell fishing?" Uncle Zack demanded.

"You did," said Big Eli, "but you didn't say anything about pearls. All you wanted was mussel shells. You've been getting them."

"I reckon you know you've been made a fool of?" Uncle Zack said.

"How so?" asked Big Eli and sat down in a chair.

Uncle Zack told what he had heard at the tavern and he knew a lot more than I did.

"If you'd have come to me in the first place, I'd have told you them mussel pearls ain't worth nothing," he said like his pride had been hurt because Big Eli went to Zybee Fletcher first.

"The whole village is abuzz about it," Miss Susie spoke up and her tone was scolding.

I saw Big Eli getting red.

"You're the laughingstock of the village," said Aunt Soph.

Uncle Zack nodded his head like he was glad the womenfolks sided with him. "Already they're calling you the man who wrote a letter to the King," he said. "And I reckon you'll never live it down."

"Or us either," said Aunt Soph and she clucked a couple of times like she did when she was scared or pestered.

For a few seconds everything was quiet. Uncle Zack and Aunt Soph and Miss Susie just looked at Big Eli waiting for him to say something but he was looking at nothing in particular, just staring and thinking. Then he started to laugh and his long yellow hair crumpled on his shoulders when he threw his head back and he rocked on the legs of his chair.

"Is that why you couldn't eat your vittles?" he asked me, and I nodded that it was.

"I heard the snake doctor telling the men at the tavern,"

I said, and Big Eli swept me in his arms and kept on laughing like it was as funny as the men at the tavern did.

Miss Susie got up and went home. I guess she couldn't understand why Big Eli was laughing so hard. Sometimes I couldn't understand Big Eli either.

CHAPTER XVIII

BIG ELI AND I went on fishing for mussel shells after that but we didn't bother saving the pearls we found now and then. Uncle Zack bought the shells from Big Eli and shipped them by keelboat to Cincinnati but I soon knew he wasn't warm to the business. I didn't know whether it was because he wasn't getting paid as much as he expected, which he wasn't, or because folks in the village were taking it out on him about the letter to the King.

Men would wink at each other when they saw him and they'd chuckle and ask him, "How's your pearl diver, Zack?" or "Sold any pearls to the King lately, Zack?" Uncle Zack would squeeze up his face and ooze out a grin, but I knew it hurt him to do it.

One night Big Eli and I went fox hunting with the Morgan brothers and when they got warmed up on cider, young Bob grinned at Big Eli and asked him, "Have you had a letter from George of late?" meaning the King, of course.

Big Eli reached over and plucked a burning chunk from the fire and tossed it into Bob's lap and Bob scampered to his feet and brushed the sparks off his britches. Everybody laughed including Big Eli and young Bob. That was the last they ever said anything to Big Eli about it. Village folks didn't say anything to Big Eli but they'd grin and wink at each other when he passed by and I knew that Big Eli saw them but he never let on he did.

One night we went to the tavern for the mail and a crowd was there waiting for the post rider to sort it out. I saw grins and winks. One man who had moved into The Purchase a month before seemed about to bust his seams trying to keep from laughing. Finally he edged over to Big Eli and everybody was watching him.

He looked up at Big Eli and grinned and I saw that he had only one front tooth and it stuck out like the tusk of a boar.

"Mister, do you want to buy a pearl?" he asked and looked around at the crowd.

"I might if it's a good one," said Big Eli.

"How could you tell if it was a good one?" the man asked.

"That's easy," said Big Eli.

I saw Big Eli's left arm swing out and around the man's neck and as it began to tighten, the man's eyes bulged and his mouth popped open. Big Eli held him like a vise and with the right hand he reached into the open mouth. Before I knew what he was up to, he yanked out the tooth. He let go and held up the tooth like he wanted to get a better look at it. The man stuck his fingers in his mouth and when he drew them out they were covered with blood.

"It's not worth the buying," Big Eli said and flicked the tooth at the man's face.

Nobody laughed and the man stood like he had been struck dumb.

The post rider began to call the mail. Uncle Zack's name was called second and Big Eli walked over and got the St. Louis paper. The crowd gave him room. After that, if there was any joking about the snake doctor making a fool of Big Eli, I never saw or heard about it.

Big Eli and I were the first people in Humility to hear about the steamboat. We were shell fishing over a sandbar when a broadhorn came up river and the crew stopped poling to rest and swap talk.

"A steamboat's coming up river in a couple of days," one of the men told me. "It's tied up at Pekin now."

"It'll be the first one up the river, won't it?" Big Eli asked and the man said it was.

"But it won't be the last," said another man, and this started talk about how steam would change everything on the river. The broadhorn men didn't like it because, they said, it would run them out of business.

"Us broadhorns and keelboaters hope she hits a snag," one of them said. "It won't stop 'em, but it might discourage 'em for a spell."

I was excited for I had never seen a steamboat. When the

broadhorn moved up river, I got Big Eli to tell me about the steamboat he had seen in Carolina before I was born. We quit fishing early that day and went home to break the news. Uncle Zack was so pleased with the news that he got out the bottle of French brandy that Big Eli had brought him. He poured drinks for Big Eli and himself, then raised his glass and held it at arm's length in front of him.

"Here's to steamboats," he said. "May we have lots of 'em!"

"The broadhorns and keelboaters don't feel that way about it," Big Eli told him.

"That bunch of pirates," said Uncle Zack. He downed his brandy. "I say it'll be good riddance to the lot of 'em."

He spent the next half hour telling how the keelboaters and broadhorns had robbed him and other shippers along the river. Steamboats, he said, would haul his tobacco to New Orleans for half the price and ten times as fast. That would mean more money in Uncle Zack's pocket, so he favored steamboats for that reason. Aunt Soph favored steamboats for another reason. She had never been to New Orleans with Uncle Zack because he said it wasn't respectable for a woman to travel by broadhorn or keelboat.

"Now I can go to New Orleans like a lady," she said, eyeing Uncle Zack like she was daring him to think up a reason why she couldn't.

After supper, Uncle Zack said he was going to the tavern to tell everybody about the steamboat coming up river in a couple of days. Aunt Soph said she wanted to tell Miss Susie about it and would go along with him. I went along too, but when we got to Miss Susie's house, Aunt Soph made Uncle Zack go inside with her and I went on to the tavern to wait for him.

The post rider's horse was at the rack and when I went in the tavern, the post rider was calling out the names of people who had mail. I had meant to break the news about the steamboat before Uncle Zack had a chance to do it, but everybody was quiet while the post keeper called the mail, so

I waited. I saw the post rider and tavern keeper with their heads together and they were looking at a letter like they were trying to make out the name or something. Both of them looked about the crowd like they hoped to see somebody in particular, and the tavern keeper saw me and whispered something to the post rider.

They motioned for me and I went to the desk.

"Where's Big Eli?" the tavern keeper asked.

"At Uncle Zack's," I said.

"Go get him," he said. "Tell him there's a letter for him."

"I'll carry it to him," I said.

The tavern keeper shook his head. "Not this letter," he said loud enough for folks around to hear him. "This is a letter from the King."

Mouths began popping open like chestnut burrs after a heavy frost. I forgot all about the steamboat and headed out to get Big Eli.

"They're topping your cotton," said Big Eli when I told him.

"No they're not," I argued. "I saw the letter myself."

That convinced him and we headed for the tavern. By that time everybody in the place knew about the letter and they opened a path for Big Eli and me to get to the desk.

"There's a letter for me, I hear," said Big Eli.

The tavern keeper nodded his head like he wasn't much surprised about it, but his hands were shaking he was so excited. "It looked important," he said, "so I thought you'd better come for it yourself."

Big Eli didn't say anything but took the letter and stuffed it in his pocket. Folks looked disappointed that he didn't open it there and we had to push our way through the crowd to get out. I took a look around but Uncle Zack hadn't got there and was still chinning at Miss Susie's about steamboats.

When we fetched up at home, Big Eli held the letter near the turpentine lamp before he opened it. In the upper left hand corner was a lion and a unicorn and under them were some words I couldn't read. Big Eli said it was the royal seal

and the words were Latin which he couldn't read either. Big
Eli's name was written in glossy black ink and after it was
the word, "Esquire."

"But Uncle Zack's the squire," I said, thinking the letter
might, after all, be for him.

Big Eli laughed. "Esquire's a word of courtesy betwix
gentlemen," he explained as he ripped open the envelope. He
took out the thick white note paper and spread it on the table
under the lamp.

"Is it from the King?" I asked.

"No, but it's from the King's chamberlain," said Big Eli.
He saw I didn't understand and he explained that a King's
chamberlain was a man who looked after the King's chores,
such as writing letters.

"What about the pearls?" I asked.

"I'll read it to you," he said, and proceeded.

Dear Mr. Wakefield.

   His Majesty has asked me to acknowledge receipt of your
letter of recent date and to inform you that, at present, his
collection of pearls is quite adequate. However, if at any time
in the future, his Majesty should be in the market for pearls
such as you describe, he requests me to assure you that he will
communicate with you. His Majesty wishes you success and
good health.

Big Eli folded the letter and put it back in the envelope,
but there was no sign of disappointment on his face.

"So they were right after all," I said, meaning Miss Susie
and Uncle Zack and all the others who said the snake doctor
had made a fool of Big Eli.

"They need never know what was in the letter if we don't
tell," he said.

"I won't tell," I said, "but the tavern keeper will tell everybody you got it."

"Let him," said Big Eli, and he looked at the clock on the
mantel. It was almost nine. He turned and faced me.

"Would you like a ride on a steamboat?" he asked.

I didn't see what a steamboat had to do with the King's

letter, but I knew Big Eli wouldn't have asked me if he didn't have something in mind. "I'd admire to," I said.

"Then let's go before Uncle Zack and Aunt Soph come back home," he said.

"Go where?" I asked.

"To Pekin," he said. "We'll go in our boat. With a nine-mile current behind us we should be there before daybreak."

We shoved into the Big River an hour later with the moonlight spread like a blanket of silver all around us. Big Eli braced the oars against the current and stopped the boat when we got over the mussel beds. He reached into his pocket and brought out the poke of pearls. He upended it into the palm of his hand and studied them a spell then he held his hand over the side of the boat and opened his fingers. The pearls slid into the water, making a rustling sound like a big moccasin easing off a limb into a swamp. Then Big Eli began to row but it wasn't until he began to sing in time with the oars that I closed my eyes and dropped off to sleep in the stern.

It was still dark and the moon had paled when we first saw the shore lights of Pekin downriver. We couldn't make out the steamboat at first but when we did sight her pilot lights, Big Eli nosed our boat into shore. We pulled it up the bank under the branches of a big oak tree that had been topped by high water during the flood. It couldn't be seen from there. By the time we walked to the landing where the steamboat was tied up, day was beginning to break. Water birds were setting up a racket in the canebrakes and black men were chopping wood while other black men lugged it aboard the steamboat. Big Eli and I stood around the landing and looked at the steamboat, which was a stern wheeler with two decks and two smokestacks. She heaved with the wash of the current and her shore lines groaned under the strain like the hub of an ox cart that needed greasing.

I nearly jumped out of my boots when, at six o'clock, there was a great hissing of steam and the boat whistle shook the air with a blast that could be heard for miles. Big flocks of ducks and geese, feeding in the canebrakes and in the wild rice of the swamps, soared into the air by the thousands and circled about with an awful clatter. I reached out a hand toward Big Eli, but he didn't take it.

He looked at me and saw I was scared. "Let on like you eat a steamboat every morning for breakfast," he said.

Big Eli was like an Injun. He never let on he was scared, if he was.

Soon after the blast had split the air, people began coming out on deck and others came down from the houses in the town.

Big Eli was looking about the crowd like he expected to see somebody he knew. Soon he did. It was one of the shell buyers we had talked to when we came to Pekin aboard the broadhorn with Uncle Zack. He saw us and came up and shook hands.

"Did you bring shells to market?" the man asked.

"No," said Big Eli, "but I've got a good shell boat I'd pleasure to sell for the right price."

"Where is it?" the shell buyer asked.

"Follow me," said Big Eli and led the way back to where we had hid the boat under the overhanging oak. We pushed it into the river and the shell buyer climbed in. He rocked it fore and aft to test the balance and looked over the racks. He seemed satisfied and stepped ashore again. It didn't take them long to strike a deal and the shell buyer paid off in silver. Then he climbed in the boat again and rowed off. Big Eli and I went back to the landing. Our shell fishing days were over, and I knew it.

Big Eli jingled the coins in his pocket and said, "We'll eat breakfast aboard the boat." We walked up the sagging plank laid between the landing and the deck.

I had never seen anything like the dining room of the steamboat. It was lined with polished wood, mostly walnut with inlay and trimmings of yellow poplar. Big windows looked out over the river and I saw the ducks and geese settling down in the marshes and canebrakes again. A black man wearing an apron led us to a table and stood back of each chair as Big Eli and I sat down. Big Eli took off his hat and put it under his chair and I did too.

The black man brought a bottle and small glass and put them down in front of Big Eli. "Brandy, sir," he said, and Big Eli poured himself a dram.

"Bacon or ham with eggs, catfish or wild duck," the black man said. We both ordered wild duck as we were used to eating hog meat and catfish at Uncle Zack's. I wondered if they had shot the ducks as they flew over the boat but when I asked Big Eli about it, the black man heard me and laughed.

"No sir," he said, "our ducks come from the bayous of Louisiana. They've been on ice since we left New Orleans."

On ice. I couldn't understand it. Later I saw the icehouse on the steamboat. It was next to the galley and had thick walls packed with sawdust. Inside it were big hunks of ice which Big Eli said had been harvested at St. Louis and shipped to New Orleans in winter. With the brakes and marshes full of ducks I couldn't see the sense of going to all the trouble to bring ducks on ice from Louisiana. But it was good eating and that's what counted for we were hungry by that time.

Before we were through eating other people came in for breakfast. Most of the men wore fancy shirts and boots that shone like a buckeye. There were four or five women and they wore the prettiest dresses I had ever seen and their hair was combed fine as a filly's tail on horse swapping day.

Two of them with pink cheeks and rosy lips smiled at me and I smiled back at them, but when I turned to see if Big Eli had caught me at it, he was looking at them and smiling and there was a twinkle in his eyes. I wasn't certain then it was me they were smiling at in the first place.

He saw how red my face was, for I was blushing.

"Let on like you eat it for breakfast," he said, meaning I shouldn't blush when a pretty woman smiled at me. I guess he was used to it. I wasn't. I wondered why Hannah and Miss Susie didn't have pink cheeks and rosy lips like the two women who had smiled at us.

A man in a uniform came around before we finished eat-

ing and asked if we were going up river. Big Eli said we were
going part way, about forty miles, and paid his fare. There
was no charge for me. As we left the dining room the two
women smiled at us again and Big Eli bowed and then put on
his hat at a dude's angle when we walked through the door.
I tilted my hat back and to the side like he did.

The black roustabouts were through carrying wood
aboard and the crew was pulling in the lines, getting ready
to shove off. I could feel the engines shaking the whole boat
and I jumped again when the whistle blew and the big paddle wheel at the stern began to churn the river. The ducks
and geese roared into the sky again. We were on our way.

A lot of people, some with boys and girls, had come
aboard while we were having breakfast. Everybody, including us, stood at the rail and waved at the people on shore as
the boat backed out from the landing and swung into the current. When we couldn't see the landing any more, Big Eli
and I walked about the boat to look at it. That's when we
saw the icehouse. We also saw the engines on the first deck
and the wheel house on the top deck. The captain was in the
wheel house, but another man was steering the big wheel.

One big room had a sign, "Salon," over the door. There
was fine furniture in it and on the walls were colored pictures
of New Orleans, Memphis and three steamboats much larger
than the one we were on. At a big table in the center of the
room a group of men were playing a game which Big Eli
said was roulette. Some of the women I had seen in the dining room were watching the game. Big Eli and I joined up
with them. There was a lot of money on the table and a big
pile of gold and silver coins was stacked in front of the man
who was spinning the roulette wheel and taking the bets.

After a spell a man I had seen get on the boat at Pekin lost
several bets running. He shoved back his chair and got up
and I guessed he'd had enough of it. One of the two women
who had smiled at us said to Big Eli, "*M'sieu*, perhaps it is
your lucky day, no." She smiled and rolled her dark eyes at
him. Big Eli touched the brim of his beaver, bowed and sat
down.

I guessed she was French for she talked like a trapper we had known in the Cumberlands and he was French.

The man who ran the game called out, "Play!" and spun the wheel while the little ball swayed and danced around trying to find a spot to settle down. Big Eli reached into his jeans and brought out a couple of coins and put them on black. Red won and the man reached out his stick and dragged in Big Eli's bet. The French lady smiled at Big Eli and said, "Better luck next time, *M'sieur*." Big Eli ducked into his jeans again and put his money on black. That time he won.

"*Très bon!*" said the French lady and tossed him a kiss with the tips of her fingers.

Big Eli switched to red and won again. He stayed with the red and while he didn't have to dig into his jeans again his winnings stayed about even until we were halfway to where we were going. I got tired watching the game and went to play on deck with two boys and a girl who were going from Illinois to Tennessee to live. They asked me more questions than a lawyer in a court. Where did I live? Who did I live with? Why did I wear long hair? Why did my father wear long hair? When they asked me where my mother was I didn't answer but left them and went to the upper deck to watch the pilot miss snags and sandbars.

I had been up there for a half hour or so when the pretty French lady came up and went into the pilot house and began talking to the captain. They both turned and looked at me and then talked together again and I felt it had something to do with Big Eli. I waited until she came out, smiled at me again, and went below. I followed her. The boat was getting close to home by then. Big Eli was still playing the red. In front of him was a pile of gold and silver and he was the only one playing though the others were watching. The wheel stopped spinning and the man with the stick shoved some more coins at Big Eli.

As Big Eli picked them up I saw the man with the stick look at the pretty French lady and their eyes talked. Big Eli saw me and grinned when I looked at his money.

"Don't tell Uncle Zack where I got it," he said.

"Play!" said the man with the stick and spun the wheel.

Big Eli crooked his neck and looked through the window toward the shore.

"We're almost there," I said.

"Play!" said the man with the stick again.

Big Eli pulled his bandanna from his pocket and spread it out in front of him and pushed the pile of coins into it. Then he drew the ends of the bandanna together and tied them into strong knots.

The French lady put her little pink hand on his shoulder and opened her eyes wide as a mussel shell on hot coals. "*M'sieur*, you're not going to quit?" she asked like she might bust out crying if he did.

"*Oui*," said Big Eli and pushed his chair back. He had learned that much French from the trapper in the Cumberlands.

When he got up and turned his back to the table, I saw the French lady glance at the man with the stick again. He curled his lip into a sort of a smile, spun the wheel and called "Play!"

When we got on deck we could see people on the river bank about a quarter of a mile upstream. I could make out Uncle Zack's rig and team and the Morgan brothers' wagon and mules. There were several women with parasols. They had come to see the steamboat and I got to feeling important at the thought of walking down the gangplank with everybody looking at us and wondering how we came to be on the boat.

Big Eli turned his face upward and I did too. The boat captain was standing at the rail of the upper deck looking at us. Big Eli smiled and pointed at the people on shore, meaning that was where we wanted to get off the boat. The captain smiled and went back to the wheelhouse. Two long blasts from the whistle shook the air and scared the daylights out of the horses and mules on shore.

I saw Uncle Zack and others run toward their teams and in a matter of seconds they were struggling to keep them from running away, wagons, rigs and all. I was so interested

in what was going on I wasn't paying attention to the boat.
Then I heard Big Eli yell, "Hey!"

I turned to see what was the matter. He was looking up
at the pilot house trying to get the attention of the captain.
Then I saw that the boat was still in midstream and we were
already abreast of the people on shore. The men and women
I had seen at the roulette table were on deck, only a few feet
away, and they were laughing at Big Eli.

Big Eli screamed "Hey!" again, and I could see he was
mad.

"We don't stop here, friend," the man who ran the game
called to him. He grinned and the others laughed.

"We do," said Big Eli. He glanced at the big wheel churning the river, then at the shore as if to judge the distance.
The gamblers must have guessed what he was up to. They
started moving toward us.

Big Eli dropped the bandanna between his feet. "Look out
for the wheel," he said to me. The next thing I knew he
gripped me by the seat of the pants and the shoulder and
lifted me from the deck. "Keep afloat until I reach you," he
said and tossed me far over the rail. I spun in the air and as
I did I saw the gamblers close in on Big Eli. Then I went
under. When I came up the water was boiling all around me
but the boat had passed and I was not in danger of the paddle
wheel.

I shook the water out of my eyes and ears and began tread-
ing water and I could hear screams of women coming from
the steamboat deck. When my ears cleared the fight was still
going on. I wondered if I should try to make shore by myself. Then I saw Big Eli leap to the rail. The bandanna was
gripped in his teeth. He seemed to pause, then he saw me and
dived in.

We waded ashore a few minutes later and everybody
crowded around us.

"The boat don't stop here," said Big Eli.

"So I noticed," said Uncle Zack and he looked at the bandanna Big Eli was carrying in his hand.

Big Eli squatted down and untied the knot. Eyes opened

wide when folks saw all the money. Big Eli started shoving it into the pockets of his jeans.

"Where'd you get all that?" Uncle Zack asked.

"Wouldn't you pleasure to know," said Big Eli and he drew a steady bead on Uncle Zack with his eyes. Then he laughed.

Miss Susie sidled up to him and we headed for Uncle Zack's rig with the others trailing us.

When we got to Humility, the Morgan brothers were still with us, and they drew up their team beside Uncle Zack's rig and Anse Morgan called to Big Eli, "I've got a good bottom farm I'd pleasure to sell at the right price." He grinned and winked.

Big Eli made like he wanted to talk about the steamboat but nobody seemed interested, even Uncle Zack. I knew they hoped he would say something about the letter and the pearls.

We were soaked to the skin and had to change to dry clothes. Uncle Zack followed us into the kitchen when we went to strip. Big Eli took the money out of his pockets and tied it in the bandanna again and then he took the letter from the King's chamberlain, which was soaked, and he spread it out on the hearth so it would dry. Uncle Zack craned his neck to get a good look at it but Big Eli managed to stand betwix him and the letter so he couldn't see the writing but I knew he saw the lion and the unicorn on the envelope. That's all he wanted to see. He tore into the big room, shutting the door behind him, and I could hear him talking in a low voice to Aunt Soph and Miss Susie. In a few minutes I heard him leave for the tavern.

"Zack thinks we sold our pearls to the King," Big Eli said to me. "The tavern keeper must've told him about the letter."

"Are you going to tell him the truth?" I asked.

"He wouldn't believe me if I did," he said. "We'll let him and the others think what they please."

Big Eli was right. Nobody mentioned the letter or the pearls but it was plain they had made up their minds we had sold the pearls to the King. The next day, when we went to the tavern, people spoke respectful to Big Eli and called him Mister Eli or Mister Wakefield. They hadn't done that before. Mr. Tweedy, the cobbler, came to Uncle Zack's and measured Big Eli for a new pair of boots.

"They'll look exactly like the boots the King wears," he said, and Big Eli told him to make them up.

Miss Susie invited all of us, Big Eli, Uncle Zack, Aunt Soph and me to supper at her home two days after we got home. She was all fluttery about the vittles she put on the table and specially about a loblolly in a big bowl which was in the center of the table. After Uncle Zack said blessing, he asked what it was.

"It's suet pudding," she said. "My uncle, who used to be a hostler to the Royal Family, says suet pudding is the King's favorite dish."

I liked pudding and this one looked good with all the steam rising from it. Miss Susie piled my plate high and I pitched into it, thinking it would be sweet and spicy. I nearly choked on the first bite. It was worse than Injun stew which sometimes was made out of dog. I managed to swallow some of it and then I remembered that Big Eli had told me to always eat what was put on my plate. That was being polite, he said. I decided the only thing to do was get it down fast and I did. Miss Susie was watching me and just as I took the last bite she smiled and said, "Bless Little Eli, how he loves my cooking."

She picked up my plate and filled it again with suet pudding. I ate slow from then on.

When bedtime rolled around Aunt Soph and Uncle Zack and I went home but Big Eli stayed. I climbed into bed and Uncle Zack and Aunt Soph went to the kitchen and shut the door. But I listened.

"She's set her cap for him now," Aunt Soph said and I knew she was talking about Miss Susie and Big Eli.

"Thanks to the letter from the King," said Uncle Zack.

"My father got a personal letter from Andy Jackson once," said Aunt Soph.

"That's not like getting a letter from the King," said Uncle Zack like he was proud to be Big Eli's brother.

"I wonder how much he got for his pearls?" Aunt Soph said.

"Must be all of a thousand dollars, maybe more," said Uncle Zack.

I dropped off to sleep and didn't hear Big Eli when he came home. In the days that followed I caught a lot of talk at the tavern and the blacksmith shop. Everybody guessed at the amount Big Eli had got for the pearls, but that wasn't the important thing with them. It was the letter itself. One day the tavern keeper was talking to a stranger when we went in. He nodded his head at Big Eli and whispered to the stranger, "There's the man who got a letter from the King."

Uncle Zack never missed a chance to be seen in Big Eli's company. When the Morgan brothers got up a dance in honor of Big Eli, Uncle Zack hinted around until Anse Morgan invited him and Aunt Soph. I knew it wouldn't be any fun for me, so I stayed home with Faro.

CHAPTER XIX

MOSES had grown to a full size crow with a glossy black coat and was as gentle as Aunt Soph's Dominicker hens, only not so fat. Faro was jealous because Big Eli and I spent a lot of time playing with Moses. Moses wanted to make friends with him but couldn't and because Faro showed his teeth and growled, Moses stayed his distance most of the time. But I had noticed one thing. Faro depended on him in a way, even though he hated Moses. When Moses would get his crop full, he'd fly to the top of the big maple in the back yard and sit there. If someone was coming into the village afoot or otherwise, Moses heard it long before Faro or I did. He would start to scold and Faro would bristle and stand guard until he found out who it was.

Moses roosted in the maple at night and unless he heard somebody coming he didn't make any sound because he was afraid the big owls would get him. But many nights after I had gone to bed and everything was quiet I would hear him start to scold and Faro would go bounding off to find out who was coming up the road. I told Big Eli about it.

"Yes, a crow is an Injun's eyes and ears," he said.

I didn't understand what he meant.

"He's like a sentry," he explained. "Injuns always feed crows to keep them around close. No enemy can get near an Injun camp without the crows knowing it and sounding a warning."

I decided Faro was a smart dog to have found that out. The night they went to the dance I kept Faro in the house because I didn't want him following Big Eli and I felt safer with him close by.

They had been gone about an hour and I had blown out the candle and gone to bed when I heard Moses start to scold from the top of the big maple. Faro charged at the front door which was shut but not locked. He raised such a ruckus that

I let him out and he raced around the house two or three times, growling and snarling. Then he dashed off to the woods in back of the house and I didn't hear him any more. I remembered Big Eli's money which he had put under a floor board in the kitchen. I got up and went to see if he had taken it with him. I lifted the board and the money was there. I was trying to put the board back into place when I heard footsteps at the kitchen door. Then somebody tried to open the door, but Aunt Soph had dropped the bar across it before she left. The footsteps started around toward the front of the house and I tried to get the board back into place but it stuck and I couldn't. I knew the front door wasn't locked because I had just let Faro out that way. I was scared plenty. I picked up the bandanna with the money in it and edged toward the kitchen door, aiming to lift the bar and run but it came to me that I would be heard if I did. My foot struck the swill bucket and I remembered I had promised Aunt Soph I would empty it before I went to bed, but I had forgotten. I eased the bandanna into the swill and crawled behind Aunt Soph's stove. I heard the front door open and close and then I caught the flare of a sulphur match as it was struck in the big room. I could tell by the footsteps it was a man in there. The light flickered shadows across the kitchen floor and I knew he had lit a candle for there were two of them on the mantel over the fireplace in the big room. He began prowling around and I wanted to look and see who it was but I was afraid I'd make a noise and he would hear me.

I kept wondering what had become of Faro and I couldn't understand why he didn't come back. The man prowled the bedroom and then came into the kitchen. He must have seen the loose floorboard for I heard him fooling with it and I knew he was searching for something, likely Big Eli's money. After a while he kicked the floorboard back in place and I heard him spit a stream of tobacco juice into the swill bucket. Then he left, but I didn't come from behind the oven for quite a spell. I thought I would call some of the neighbors but decided against it as the less they knew about Big Eli's money the better. But I didn't go back to sleep.

When Big Eli and Uncle Zack and Aunt Soph came home I told what had happened. Big Eli got the Gabriel Horn and tried to blow Faro in, and when he didn't come I could see that Big Eli was worried. He thought the man had killed him, but I knew that didn't happen because I would have heard a gunshot. Big Eli and Uncle Zack questioned me about the man but I couldn't tell them much for I hadn't seen him. We went to bed and to sleep.

Right after breakfast the next morning Big Eli took his money and went to the woods. Soon he came back without it and I knew he had hid it out there somewhere.

CHAPTER XX

AFTER the Morgan dance, Big Eli began spending more time at Miss Susie's. With a good supper under his belt, he'd spruce himself up and say to me, "Don't wait up for me, Little Eli. I'll be out late." I was always asleep when he got home. Uncle Zack and Aunt Soph were mighty pleased about this.

There was no school in the village and because of that I had to read a chapter of Scripture every day from Uncle Zack's Bible. It was the biggest Bible I had ever seen. It was covered with rawhide which had been handled so much that it was soft and fuzzy and along the edges of the cover there were brass studs which protected it from wear. I had been told it was over a hundred years old and had been brought across the sea from England where Uncle Zack's people came from.

One day I overheard Aunt Soph and Uncle Zack talking in the kitchen and it was about a party to be held in Uncle Zack's barn. I tiptoed to the kitchen door but Aunt Soph heard me.

"You haven't read your Scripture task today," she said when she saw me.

"Better do it now," Uncle Zack said.

Aunt Soph shut the door in my face. I liked to read Scripture but I didn't hanker to have Aunt Soph tell me to do it. Instead of opening the Bible at the place where I had left off the day before, I opened it at a page near the front. At the top of the page were the words "Family Record." On that page was written the names of Uncle Zack's kin and the dates when they were born, married and died. My mother's name was next to Big Eli's and mine, though it only told when she married Big Eli and when she died.

I was still trying to hear what Aunt Soph and Uncle Zack had to say about the party for I knew they didn't want me to know what they were talking about. They stopped talking and I was about to look for my Scripture task when I happened to notice the date next to my name. Then I realized that in two days I would have a birthday and would be ten years old. I was about to call Uncle Zack and Aunt Soph and remind them of it and then it came to me that's why they didn't want me to hear what they were saying. The party they were talking about was to be for me and it was to be a surprise. I was glad I hadn't asked them any questions. I found my Scripture task and read it out loud so they could hear me, and when I finished I went for a long walk in the woods by myself. I wondered if I would feel any different being ten years old, or if Big Eli would let me blow the Gabriel Horn. I was afraid he wouldn't for I was a long way from being a man and he had said it took a man's wind to blow it. But I guessed I would get presents from him and Uncle Zack and Aunt Soph and maybe other people too. I felt mighty proud that they had remembered my birthday and were going to give a party so big it had to be held in Uncle Zack's warehouse. The next two days passed mighty slow for me and I spent most of my time in the woods so I wouldn't let on that I knew anything about it. When I came home to eat I noticed that Uncle Zack and Aunt Soph and Big Eli mentioned the party only when they thought I was out of earshot.

I thought Aunt Soph would bake a cake for my birthday but she didn't and I guessed she had asked Miss Susie to bake it so I wouldn't find out about it.

Just before we ate supper the night of the party, Aunt Soph heated a big iron pot of water and Big Eli and I took our ablutions and decked ourselves out in our best riggin'. It was dark by the time we sat down to eat and Aunt Soph dished up the usual fare without any special fixings. I thought Uncle Zack might mention my birthday in his blessing but he didn't. After we ate, Uncle Zack lit the lantern and left for the warehouse and Aunt Soph started clearing the dishes.

"You can dry them for me," she said.

Big Eli patted me on the back and said, "You've got a big surprise coming tonight, Little Eli." I made out like I didn't know a thing and he left for Miss Susie's.

Before Aunt Soph and I got through with the kettles and the dishes I could hear people riding by on horseback and in rigs and wagons. Moses was raising plenty of ruckus from the top of the big elm tree and Faro was trying to whip all the strange dogs that had come along with their folks to the party. After the dishes and kettles were put away, Aunt Soph told me to go into the big room while she took her ablutions. In a spell she came out and she had on the dress Big Eli had bought her in Tennessee. She looked mighty sweet and I was right proud when she took hold of my arm, like I was Uncle Zack, and we left for the party.

We found the place almost full of people. Lanterns were hanging all over and three fiddlers were sitting on top of a hogshead playing for all they were worth and banging their bootheels to the time of the music.

Aunt Soph stopped at the door where Uncle Zack was shaking hands like a politician. I saw the Morgan men and their womenfolks and went to talk to them. They were glad to see me but nobody said anything about it being my birthday or me being ten years old. I guessed Big Eli must have told them it was going to be a surprise and he wanted to tell me himself.

The fiddlers had stopped playing when I heard Uncle Zack call out, "Here they come!"

Everybody turned toward the big doors and the fiddlers started bearing down and beating their heels to the music. I saw Big Eli and Miss Susie come through the open doors and everybody began to cheer and clap hands. Then Uncle Zack grabbed Miss Susie and started dancing and Big Eli swung Aunt Soph into his arms and began to dance too while everybody followed suit. I stood by the big hogshead next to the fiddlers and watched and wondered when somebody would begin to pay attention to me. After a few turns, Big Eli and Uncle Zack swapped partners and as he and Miss Susie swayed past me, Big Eli gave me a wink and a big grin.

I had never seen Miss Susie so pretty and she was smiling and laughing like she was enjoying dancing with Big Eli. She didn't smile and laugh as a usual habit. Her black hair was drawn back tight from her forehead and done up in a big knot at the back and in the knot was a comb that spread out like a peacock's tail and it glittered in the light of the lanterns. It made her look taller than she was and she was a tall woman. But even then she looked small beside Big Eli.

The music stopped and everybody began to clap hands and cheer. Big Eli and Miss Susie came and stood beside me, though they paid me no heed. Uncle Zack raised his hand to quiet things down and when it did he stepped out a couple of paces onto the floor where everybody could see him. Aunt Soph smiled at Miss Susie and Miss Susie waved her hand at Aunt Soph.

"Ladies and gentlemen," I heard Uncle Zack saying in a high pitched voice like a snake doctor selling herb cures. He paused to let things get quieter before he went on.

Big Eli cupped his hand over my shoulder and smiled down at me and whispered, "Here comes the surprise, Little Eli."

Uncle Zack cleared his throat. "At this time, ladies and gentlemen," he said, "it brings me great pleasure to announce the engagement of my esteemed brother, Elias Wakefield, to a lovely and charming lady of this community, Miss Susie Spann."

Everybody cheered and Miss Susie and Big Eli beamed at the folks about them.

"It is for that reason you have been invited here tonight," Uncle Zack started out again.

I don't remember what else he said. People began rushing toward us. The men shook hands with Big Eli and the women kissed Miss Susie and tears began to run down Aunt Soph's cheeks. Tears were crowding to my eyes too, but not for the same reason. I knew by then the party was not to celebrate my birthday, and I knew why Aunt Soph hadn't baked a cake. My birthday had been forgotten completely. The fiddlers started playing again. Big Eli took Miss Susie in his arms, kissed her, and then swung her out on the floor.

Everybody clapped hands and began to dance. I headed for the door.

A hundred thoughts were whirling in my head to the time of the music when I reached the black night outside. I wondered if this was what Big Eli had tromped all the way from the Cumberlands for. Uncle Zack had written to Big Eli that The Purchase was a paradise for the hunter, but I knew Miss Susie had bagged Big Eli without firing a shot. He was the hunted, she was the hunter. If I hadn't liked her before, I liked her less now. I wondered if I was beginning to hate Big Eli.

I heard footsteps behind me and I turned to see if it was him, but it was too dark to make out who it was. Then I heard a man say, "Wait up for me, Little Eli?" It was Bob Morgan, but I didn't stop and he upped his pace and came beside me. "What's the matter, boy?" he asked.

"I won't tell you," I said.

"Yes you will," he said, and laid his hand on my shoulder. "Something happened back there. What was it?"

I liked Bob Morgan and I knew he liked me. I had to tell somebody or break down crying.

"It's my birthday," I said.

"Your birthday?" he said, like he didn't understand.

"I thought the party was going to be for me," I said.

He stopped dead in his tracks and I stopped too.

"I'll be a sonofagun," he said, then asked, "Didn't Big Eli know it was your birthday?"

"He forgot about it," I said.

"Let's go back and remind him," Bob said and yanked my arm and I knew he was mad. I jerked away from him.

"No, I won't go back," I said.

Moses was scolding from the top of the Big Elm and Faro was fighting with strange dogs up the road.

"Then I'll go with you, and we'll have a birthday party all our own, Little Eli," Bob Morgan said. We started again toward the house. We were almost to the door when I saw the flickering light through the window. I remembered that Aunt Soph had blown out the candles before we left and I wondered if it might be from the fireplace. But the light moved and I knew it was either a match or a candle.

I stopped and whispered, "Somebody's in there!"

"Who?" Bob asked.

"I don't know," I said, and I remembered the man who had tried to find Big Eli's money before.

"I'll find out," he said and we moved toward the door, making no sound. Bob opened the door with a jerk and went inside and I followed behind him. Stan Bodine wheeled to face us, holding a candle in his hand.

The bricks in the fireplace where Uncle Zack hid his money were laying on the hearth and the secretary desk had been ransacked and papers were scattered on the floor.

"You, Morgan," Bodine said and stuck the lighted candle on the mantel.

"What're you doing here, Bodine?" Bob asked him.

Bodine didn't answer and his fat face turned evil.

"Go get Big Eli," Bob said to me, but before I started Bodine said, "No need for that!" Then he stepped a pace toward Bob Morgan.

"Morgan," he said, "you butted into my business once before." I knew he was talking about the time Bob jerked the bull whip out of his hand. "You've butted in the last time," said Bodine.

I saw the knife flash as it came out of his pocket and he held it point first at chest level and lunged. Bob Morgan tried to sidestep, but Bodine was big and fast on his feet. For a second they grappled and then I saw Bob slide to the floor and roll over his back. Bodine still had the knife in his hand when I ran screaming through the door. I heard his fast footsteps behind me and I thought he was trying to catch me, but he wasn't. Before I got to the warehouse I heard him mount and ride off cussing the horse.

The fiddlers were playing a hoedown and the men were stomping their boots and I had to yell at the top of my voice to be heard, and when they saw my scared face everything stopped as sudden and still as death.

"Stan Bodine's knifed Bob Morgan!" I yelled and pointed to the dark outside.

The men didn't wait for more talk. They bolted for the door, but Uncle Zack took time to grab a lantern as he ran.

"Where is he?" Big Eli asked me as we ran outside.

"In the house," I said, and Big Eli yelled to the others, "In the house!"

Big Eli and the Morgan brothers were the first inside and Uncle Zack followed with the lantern and held it over Bob. Anse Morgan and Big Eli knelt down beside Bob and Anse tore away the shirt which was covered with blood. Big Eli felt Bob's pulse and leaned an ear against the bloody chest to hear a heart beat.

When he straightened up, he said, "He's dead."

"Knifed in the heart," said Anse and looked at his brothers.

Big Eli turned to me. "Did Bodine leave afoot or astride?"

I said, "Astride. I heard him ride off in that direction." I pointed west.

"Get him, men," Big Eli said and the men, except Big Eli, Uncle Zack and Anse Morgan started for their horses.

The women came in excited and some of them weeping. Bob Morgan's girl pushed through and looked at him, then swooned.

"Get the brandy, Sophia," Uncle Zack said and picked up the girl and took her to the bedroom. Aunt Soph got the brandy bottle off the shelf and followed him and so did some of the other women. Big Eli lit the turpentine lamp and the room was filled with light.

Uncle Zack came back and started to question me how it happened, but Big Eli interrupted him. "Never mind, Zack," he said, "let's get Bob out of here and lay him out in the warehouse."

Uncle Zack handed me the lantern. He and Big Eli and Anse Morgan lifted Bob from the floor and carried him to the warehouse which was empty and our footsteps made a hollow sound as we trod across the floor. Uncle Zack put two meeting benches together and Anse and Big Eli laid Bob down and Anse folded his brothers arms over his chest. Then he sat down beside Bob and cried. Uncle Zack whispered a prayer and Big Eli just stared at Bob and his chest heaved.

When Uncle Zack quit praying, Big Eli said, "Zack, keep the women out of here." He started to move away.

"Where're you going?" Uncle Zack asked him.

"Bodine may head for his place," Big Eli said. "I'm riding up there." He stalked out. I went back to the house but didn't go in for the women were weeping and praying.

I heard Big Eli ride out of the horse lot and he drew up at the door. "Get my rifle," he said, and I went in and got it. The women stared at me when they saw me with the gun but I paid no heed and went outside and handed it to Big Eli. He touched a bootheel to the flank of the horse and was gone into the night.

I stood there thinking how I would remember my tenth birthday the rest of my life.

CHAPTER XXI

BY DAYBREAK most of the men came back. They hadn't found a trace of Stan Bodine. Uncle Zack and the Morgan men were starting to fret about Big Eli and there was talk of riding up to Bodine's place to look for him. Before they got started, Big Eli rode in with the Sheriff and Doc Haney, the coroner.

"He didn't go home," Big Eli said as he slid out of the saddle.

"Did you talk to his woman?" Uncle Zack asked.

Big Eli nodded. "Yes," he said, and I knew he had said all he was going to for the time.

Doc Haney and the Sheriff dismounted, and Doc asked where the body was. Tully Morgan took him to the warehouse and I followed along with the Sheriff and Big Eli. The other men had gone there ahead of us. Doc looked at the wound in Bob's chest, and then turned to Big Eli. "You say the boy was the only witness?" he asked.

"Yes," said Big Eli. "Tell Doc and the Sheriff how it happened, Little Eli," he said to me.

I did, and when I told what Bodine said to Bob about butting into his business once before, Doc and Sheriff Foster didn't understand. Big Eli told them about the fight he had with Bodine and how Bob Morgan had jerked the whip out of Bodine's hand. Two or three men in the crowd had seen it happen and they backed up what Big Eli said.

"So he squared things with Bob last night," said Big Eli. "Now I've got to square things with Bob."

Everybody looked at him, wondering what he meant.

Big Eli looked at the Sheriff. "You can post a bounty of a thousand dollars for Bodine," he said. "I'll pay it."

In a little while the Sheriff got on his horse and rode off toward Wadesboro, but Doc Haney, who didn't live so far, stayed to help build a coffin for Bob. When it was done and

Bob was laid in it, the men began hitching their teams and gathering up their womenfolks to go home.

When they were gone, Aunt Soph started cooking breakfast and Big Eli scrubbed the bloodstains off the floor in the big room. Then he and I washed up while Aunt Soph put the vittles on the table. I was hungry and I couldn't understand why I was.

"Did you see his woman?" Aunt Soph asked.

Big Eli nodded.

"How did she take the news?" Aunt Soph asked.

"She didn't have much to say," Big Eli said, and Aunt Soph knew by the way he said it she wasn't going to get any more out of him. She sat down to eat, and after a spell she spoke again, but not to ask a question.

"Now Bodine's cleared out," she said, "I reckon she'll be traipsing after him when he lets her know where he is."

"You reckon," said Big Eli, like Aunt Soph was allowed to have her own opinion but it wasn't his. We ate the rest of the breakfast in silence.

The next day they buried Bob Morgan and Uncle Zack preached the funeral.

He quoted Scripture which said it was wrong to kill and those who had killed would pay the penalty come judgment day. He was trying to tell the Morgan brothers and Big Eli that they should let God take care of Stan Bodine. I doubted if they would if they got the chance to do it themselves.

That night I lay awake a long time thinking about Hannah living back in the hills by herself and wondering what she would do, now that she didn't have a man to look after her. I wondered what she would do if Big Eli did kill Stan Bodine. I hoped the Morgans or the Sheriff would get Bodine before Big Eli had a chance to kill him. I didn't want her to hate Big Eli.

CHAPTER XXII

UNCLE ZACK liked fancy shirts with pearl buttons on them.
About a month after Bob Morgan had been buried, Aunt
Soph washed two of Uncle Zack's shirts and hung them on
a line in the back yard to dry in the sun. I had gone with Big
Eli and Uncle Zack to the bottoms where they looked over
a piece of land that Uncle Zack owned. They didn't say why
they wanted to look it over but from what they said to each
other I soon knew they were looking for a likely spot to
build a house. That house, I knew, would be ours when
Big Eli married Miss Susie Spann. They agreed on a wooded
knoll which wouldn't be under water at flood time, because
the river was not far off.

"I'll build a landing down yonder," said Uncle Zack pointing toward the river. "You'll be right handy to take care of
loading tobacco when steamboats tie up."

Big Eli agreed it was a likely place to build a house because
there was plenty of timber to use without hauling it. Then
we went back to Humility, and when we got there Aunt
Soph was as mad as I had ever seen her. She shook her finger
at me.

"Little Eli," she said, "you've got to get shed of that crow
or I will!"

"What's Moses done?" I asked her.

She went into the kitchen and brought back the shirts she
had washed and hung on the line to dry. "Look at these," she
said, holding them out so Big Eli and Uncle Zack could see
them.

They were smeared with muddy crow tracks, and I almost
laughed. Uncle Zack was the first to notice that the pearl
buttons were gone.

"Where are the buttons?" he asked.

"That crow ate them!" snapped Aunt Soph.

I saw Big Eli quench a smile, but it wasn't funny to Uncle Zack. "That crow's a dadblasted nuisance!" he shouted.

"I'd have wrung his neck if I'd have caught him," said Aunt Soph. "These shirts are ruined complete."

"A crow on the wing is bad enough, but a pet crow is worse," Uncle Zack said. "I don't see why you saved the critter's life in the first place."

"You've got to kill him, Elias," Aunt Soph said to Big Eli. "I won't have him around here any more."

I started to protest but Big Eli lifted a hand to stop me. "I'll talk it over with Little Eli," he said, looking at Aunt Soph and Uncle Zack. Aunt Soph grunted something I couldn't make out and went back to the kitchen with the dirty shirts and Uncle Zack followed her to look out the back door and crane his neck for Moses.

"You won't kill him, will you?" I asked Big Eli.

"There's no need to kill him," Big Eli said, "but we'll have to get shed of him."

"What will we do with him?" I asked.

"Take him to the bottoms and let him go free," he said. "So catch him up in the morning when you feed him."

Big Eli had changed since coming to The Purchase and I blamed Uncle Zack and Aunt Soph and Miss Susie for it. He had always sided with me but now he was knuckling under to Aunt Soph and Uncle Zack. Big Eli knew I loved Moses, and I remembered something he had said about crows.

"Make a pet of a crow and you make an outcast," he had told me. "His kind will shun him like pestilence ever after."

That meant Moses could never go back to the wild again. Other crows would know he had been around humans and wouldn't have anything to do with him. I thought how lonesome I would be if that happened to me.

"I'll get shed of him myself," I told Big Eli, and my throat got tight.

He looked at me and his eyes softened. "I reckon you'll feel better about it if you do," he said.

"Tomorrow," I promised.

The next morning Moses was squalling for his breakfast at the back door when I got up. I hurried into my riggin' for fear Uncle Zack might take a notion in his head to kill him. He was easy to catch but he squawked plenty when I stuffed him into a tow sack so I could carry him away without hurting him. After I ate, Big Eli saddled one of Uncle Zack's mules and shortened the stirrups. I mounted from a stump and the mule shied when Big Eli handed me the sack with Moses in it. He had a reason to. Moses had pestered the mule by flying around him and then settling down on the middle of his backbone. The mule would buck and back his ears and try to bite, but he couldn't reach Moses. Then the mule would try to knock Moses off with his tail but that didn't work either. That's why he shied when Big Eli passed the sack up to me and the mule heard Moses scolding inside it.

I tightened the rein and heeled the mule into a trot toward the bottoms and Big Eli watched me out of sight.

I rode for nearly a mile through the woods before I thought it was safe to turn off the road and head south. It was almost an hour later that I rode into the clearing and I could see a potlicker dog sleeping on the porch, but she heard us and jumped up and raced toward us barking and snarling. Somewhere, I knew, I had seen that dog. Then I remembered the bitch that we saw in front of Uncle Zack's house the morning after the robber tried to find Big Eli's money. This was her.

Hannah came to the door and saw who it was. She called off the potlicker. I reined up the mule and slid out of the saddle and she ran down the porch steps and before I could say anything, hugged and kissed me and I saw tears in her eyes.

"Little Eli!" she kept saying and then she would hug and kiss me again. Finally she asked, "Do they know you've come here?"

"No, they don't," I said.

"Why did you come?" she asked me, and I held out the tow sack with Moses in it. The mule snorted and backed off.

Hannah looked startled when she saw the sack move like it was alive. I laughed. "I've got a pet crow for you," I said.

She looked puzzled.

"You need him," I said.

She laughed. "Why do I need a pet crow?" she asked.

I had remembered what Big Eli told me after the man had tried to steal his money.

"A crow is an Injun's eyes and ears," I said. "Nobody can come around here without him knowing about it long before you do. He'll warn you."

The potlicker was sniffing the sack and growling.

Hannah hugged me again.

"His name's Moses," I said. "You'd better keep him in a chicken coop a few days until he gets used to you."

We went to look for one and the potlicker followed us, sniffing and showing her teeth. I guessed she didn't like Moses any better than Faro did. We found a coop in the back yard and put Moses in it, then we went into the house and Hannah asked me to tell her all I knew about the killing of Bob Morgan.

"Big Eli didn't know much to tell when he was here," she said.

I started out by telling her about the party in Uncle Zack's warehouse and how I thought it was a birthday party for me. When I told how disappointed I was when I found out it was for Big Eli and Miss Susie and how I had left to go to Uncle Zack's house, she put her arm around me and buried her face in the hair of my neck. "Poor boy," she said. Then I wished I hadn't told her about Big Eli's and Miss Susie's being engaged, but she knew about it anyway.

"Stan told me about the party," she said. "He taunted me all that day about it."

"Taunted you?" I repeated, not knowing why he would do that.

She didn't answer right off. "Yes," she finally said. "Stan had heard that Big Eli offered to marry me the night we got to The Purchase. He thought I was in love with him. He never would believe that Big Eli only offered to wed me to keep me out of trouble."

She got up and walked to the door. "You'd better go now,

Little Eli," she said. "They'll be wondering where you are."

I followed her to the porch. I didn't know what to say, so I said, "When you hear Moses scold quiet like from the tree tops night or day you'll know somebody's prowling around. He'll be your sentry."

"I'm glad to know that," she said. "Somebody's been prowling around most every night since the killing."

"Him?" I asked, meaning Bodine.

"No," she said. "I doubt if he'll ever come back."

I led the mule to a stump and climbed into the saddle, then I headed back the way I had come, entering the village from the direction of the bottoms. Big Eli saw me and came to meet me at the lot gate. When I slid out of the saddle he said, "You went a far piece with Moses."

"I didn't want him to find his way back here," I said, and from the way Big Eli looked at me I was certain he knew I wasn't telling all I knew.

CHAPTER XXIII

Miss Susie Spann ate Sunday dinner with us and most of the talk was about the new house and where it was to be built.

"Let's ride down and have a look at the place," Uncle Zack said, and Miss Susie and Aunt Soph agreed it was a good idea.

"After all, you're going to live there," Aunt Soph said to Miss Susie.

Uncle Zack hitched his trotters to his rig and the five of us piled in. It was a nice day and the horses took it easy over the rough road. Uncle Zack let Big Eli handle the team and Miss Susie sat in the front seat with him. I sat between Uncle Zack and Aunt Soph on the back seat. When we got there Uncle Zack explained things to Miss Susie.

"Down yonder will be the boat landing," he said. "I'm going to build a freight shed there to house my bales until they're picked up by the steamboats."

Miss Susie said she thought it would be exciting to live near the river again like she had when she was a girl in New Orleans.

"Elias can be close at hand to deal with the boat captains," Uncle Zack went on. "With him handling the freighting end of the business, I can spend more time with the growers."

Everything seemed agreeable to Miss Susie.

"When will you start building our house?" she asked Big Eli.

"When I know what kind of a house you want," said Big Eli.

"It'll be modest at first," said Uncle Zack, "but it can grow . . ." He started to say something else but Aunt Soph gave him a look that shut him up.

Miss Susie blushed and smiled at him. "I'm going to insist on one luxury, Squire," she said.

Uncle Zack asked, "What is it?"

"A bay window like the one you have in your house," she

said. Uncle Zack bobbed his head about like a gobbler dodging an axe. "Don't see why not, Miss Susie," he said. Uncle Zack was proud of his bay window which was the only one in Humility.

"When I see a bay window in a house," Miss Susie said, smearing it thick, "I always say quality folks live there."

Uncle Zack chuckled. "You say such nice things, Miss Susie," he said.

Big Eli glanced at the sun which was getting low and said, "We'd better start back." Miss Susie held out her hand and he histed her to the front seat of the rig. Uncle Zack helped Aunt Soph into the back seat and then he and I climbed in. Big Eli eased into the seat beside Miss Susie and the horses, hungry for their supper, legged it home at a fancy trot that must have shook up Uncle Zack's liver.

That night everything was house talk. There was to be a big room with an attic and I was to sleep in the attic. There would be a bedroom and a lean-to for the kitchen and dining room. The bay window was to face the river.

"So I can see Elias working," said Miss Susie and laughed.

"You'd better keep an eye on him," said Aunt Soph and though she chuckled when she said it, I guessed she meant it.

"I'll send to Pittsburg right off for the bay window glass," Uncle Zack said and Miss Susie pinched his ear.

The next day Big Eli and I went to the bottoms and began felling timber. I helped trim off the limbs and skin the bark so it would season quicker. It took almost three weeks to cut and trim enough logs of the right size and for a few days we had a hired man to help us. Measuring, sawing and notching the logs came next and after that was done Big Eli felled a big cypress and sawed it into shingle lengths. We spent another week with a wedge and a maul and a froe splitting and trimming shingles which we laid out in the sun to dry and season straight. At night, after supper, Big Eli worked in Uncle Zack's warehouse making the doors and window frames from sawed lumber he bought at a saw mill. At the end of the fifth week everything was ready for the raising.

Uncle Zack set the date and passed the word around and

the women began cooking up vittles which included cakes and pies. It was decided not to have a dance after the raising because Big Eli didn't think it fitting to the memory of Bob Morgan. There were more than twenty men on hand to help us, including Anse and Terry and Tully Morgan. They cut long poles with forks at the end and used them to lift the logs into place. Because Big Eli and I had notched the timber, the work went fast and each log fitted into place. By noon the walls were up and the rafters set and pegged. The Morgan brothers had brought jugs of cider which only the men drank and by the time they started nailing shingles to the roof, Uncle Zack was so unsteady on his feet that Big Eli made him take a nap in the shade. Long before sundown the heavy work was done, leaving only the floor and the doors and the bay window to be done by Big Eli and me. Then the raising party broke up and everybody went home.

After supper that night, Big Eli scrubbed up, put on his courting duds and went to call on Miss Susie. Uncle Zack got the Bible and read scripture to me and Aunt Soph. It was the part about Samson and Delilah and how Samson lost his strength when Delilah cut off his long hair. I was tired when he quit reading and shucked my riggin' and climbed into bed.

It must have been long after midnight when I had the dream. I saw Big Eli fighting with Stan Bodine, just like he had fought him that day when Bob Morgan jerked the bull whip out of Bodine's hand. Big Eli was giving Bodine the beating of his life, and then I saw Miss Susie Spann. She had a long pair of shears in her hand and kept trying to catch up to Big Eli. Every time he got near her she would reach out with the shears. I tried to yell and tell him but I couldn't make a sound. Then I saw her clip his hair and the long curls rolled down his back and fell in the mud where Stan Bodine trampled on them. Then Big Eli seemed to change from a big man, broad, tall and strong to a puny man like Uncle Zack. Stan Bodine was laughing at him.

I woke up then, all covered with sweat, and realized Big Eli had come home and was sound asleep next to me. For a long time I lay still, thinking of my dream but it seemed so real I had to make certain it was a dream after all. I didn't want to wake Big Eli because he would want to know why I did, but I had to know if he still had his long hair. I slipped a hand toward his head on the pillow and my fingers touched hair that was short and stiff, not long and soft. I drew my hand away when he changed the pace of his breathing. I knew I must be mistaken. I tried to go back to sleep but couldn't.

His breathing leveled off. I reached out my hand again and this time there was no doubt about it. His hair was short. It had been cut that night and I knew who had cut it and I hated her. Mine, I thought, would be next but I swore then and there that she would never get the chance. I sneaked over the foot of the bed so not to wake Big Eli. I put on my riggin' but not my boots for I was afraid Big Eli might hear me as I left. I carried them in my hand until I got outside.

I was putting them on when Faro's cold nose touched my hand and I scratched behind his ears to keep him quiet. Then it struck me that Big Eli would try to find me and that he would set Faro on my scent, come morning. I went around to the back of the house where Uncle Zack had hung a bunch of onions to dry in the sun. I pulled one of the biggest from the bunch and split it with my pocket knife. Then I rubbed the onion over the soles of my boots and stuffed it into my pocket to use again later on. When I started off Faro wanted to follow me and I had to pick up a stick and run him back. Then I set off at an Injun trot through the woods.

CHAPTER XXIV

DAY BROKE before I got there and the sun rose red through the mist over the river and the hills. Before I could see the house, a thin streak of blue smoke snaked up through the trees and I knew she was fixing breakfast. I heard the potlicker barking and wondered how she had heard me from that distance and then I remembered Moses. I knew he had squawked a warning which set off the bitch. As I came into the clearing the potlicker ran toward me, barking and snarling. Hannah was standing in the door and when she saw who it was she called off the dog, which followed at a pace, sniffing and growling.

"What on earth fetches you here this time of day?" Hannah asked when I came up.

"I've run off," I said.

"Run off?" she repeated.

"I'm never going back there," I told her.

She steadied a look at me but she didn't laugh.

"Breakfast is ready," she said. "There's enough for both of us."

She set another plate at the table and put more eggs and hog meat in the frying pan. When they were done she filled my plate and sat down across the table from me.

"Now let's hear about it," she said and I began to eat and talk. Between bites I told her about the dream and how, when I woke up, I found it was all true and that Big Eli's long hair had been cut. She didn't say anything while I told her the story, but when I finished she threw back her red head and began to laugh like it was the funniest thing she had ever heard. I thought she was laughing at me and she must have known I did.

"I'm not laughing at you, Little Eli," she said.

"What are you laughing at?" I asked.

"At him," she said and started laughing again. "Delilah cut Samson's hair," she kept repeating as she laughed.

"She'll never cut mine," I said. "That's why I ran away."

After a spell she quit laughing and said, "He'll come after you, Little Eli."

"He don't know where I am," I said.

"He'll trail you with the dog, for there's a heavy dew this morning," she said.

"The dog can't trail me," I said, and pulled the onion out of my pocket. "I smeared onion on the soles of my boots."

She laughed again.

"You can't make me go back," I told her.

"I don't aim to try," she said. "You can stay here as long as you please."

"I hate her," I said. She looked at me but didn't say anything and began clearing the dishes from the table.

"While I wash the dishes, would you feed the stock for me?" she asked and I said I would. I was glad to be of help to Hannah.

I went to the stable and fed the two mules and three hogs. I had seen a cow in the lot when I was there before but she was gone and so were Stan Bodine's horses. I looked in the shed and his fancy rig was gone too. His work wagon was still there. When I got back to the house I asked her about the cow and horses and rig.

"A man took them for debt," she said.

Moses was squawking for his breakfast at the back door. I asked for a biscuit and she gave it to me. When I went outside Moses flew to my shoulder and scolded until I crumbled the biscuit and he ate from my hand.

"He hasn't forgotten you," said Hannah who was watching from the door.

"He heard me coming here this morning and set off the potlicker," I told her.

"I heard him," she said. "I knew somebody was coming long before I saw who it was."

While she swept the floor I got a spade and dug worms for Moses. It didn't take long to fill his crop and he flew to the top branches of the sycamore that Stan Bodine had left standing in the front yard. Hannah was singing as she worked about the house and I sat in the kitchen door and listened to her. Later on I drew water for her and she began cooking. When the sun was noon high we sat down to eat again. We had just finished and started clearing the dishes when I heard Moses scold from his perch in the sycamore. The potlicker had been asleep on the porch but she came to life and went racing down the path that I had followed that morning.

"Somebody's coming," I said.

"Let's see who it is," she said, and we both went to the front door. Nobody was in sight but from the way the potlicker was barking I knew there would be soon. Then I saw Faro come out of the timber and a few seconds later Big Eli appeared.

"He's come for you, Little Eli," Hannah said.

"I'll not go back," I said. "You've got to hide me."

She pushed me behind her so Big Eli couldn't catch sight of me. "Get behind the door and don't make a sound," she said. "I'll get shed of him."

I did as she told me, but I watched through the crack of the door. Hannah was standing betwix us and I couldn't see Big Eli until he came up to her and touched the brim of his beaver with his fingers. Then I couldn't believe what I saw. He had his hair, long and curling over his shoulders just like it had always been. And he wasn't puny like I saw him in the dream, but was big and strong. I couldn't understand it.

"Where is he?" I heard him ask Hannah.

"I haven't seen him since it happened," she said, and for the second I didn't understand what she meant. Neither did Big Eli.

"Seen who since what happened?" he asked, his brow puckering in wonderment.

"Bodine," she said, and then I knew she was trying to throw him off my scent.

Big Eli shook his head. "I'm not after Bodine," he said. "I'm after Little Eli."

"Little Eli?" she repeated, and then asked, "Why would he come here?"

"He came here once before," Big Eli said, and I wondered how he knew.

"What makes you think so?" Hannah asked.

He tilted his head and pointed to the top of the big syca-more where Moses was still scolding. "He brought the crow here," he said and a smile broke over his face. "Didn't he?"

She didn't answer right off. "It's no cause he should come again," she finally said and her voice was unfriendly. Then she said, "Your woman wouldn't like it if she knew you came here."

She was talking about Miss Susie. For a second the smile left Big Eli's face and his skin reddened.

"No woman tells me where I go," he said.

Hannah laughed like she did when I told her about the dream. "Someday she'll cut that pretty long hair of yours," she told him, "and she'll put a ring in your nose so you can't stray off like this."

She laughed like Beelzebub enjoying the torments of sin-ners.

Big Eli flexed his fingers and I wondered if he was going to hit her, and I couldn't have blamed him if he had. But he didn't. I knew he was trying to make up his mind about something. All of a sudden he reached out. His left arm went about her waist and he drew her tight against him while his right hand tilted her red head back and he bent his face down against hers and kissed her on the lips time after time. At first she didn't seem to mind, but when he didn't let go she strug-gled and broke away, slapping him across the face as she did.

"Get out of here!" she screamed at him. "Get out!"

He only laughed at her.

I felt something cold against my sweating left hand and looked down to see what it was. It was Faro's nose. I had been so took up with what I saw through the crack in the door that I hadn't seen him come through the kitchen. I tried to push him away, but he began to bark and when I glanced through the crack in the door I saw Hannah trying to get between it and Big Eli.

Big Eli laughed. "Flush him out, Faro," I heard him call and I knew my game was up. I walked out with Faro licking my face and hands, and I recollected the Scripture about how Judas kissed Jesus after he betrayed him.

Big Eli watched me with a strange smile as I walked out on the porch. Faro was barking like he thought he had done something smart.

"Why did you run away?" Big Eli asked me.

I set my jaw to keep from crying, for I knew I could never tell him about the dream. Finally I asked, "Who slept in our bed last night?"

Big Eli looked puzzled. "A man from Texas," he said. "The tavern was full up and I brought him home after you went to sleep." I could see he was still wondering why I had run away, but I was not going to tell him. He waited for me to say something and when I didn't, Hannah asked him, "Does the man from Texas crop his hair?"

Big Eli must have thought she was taunting him for his eyes flashed mad when he looked at her. But her face told him she wasn't and then he must have seen the light for he looked at me again and laughed big. "The man from Texas crops his hair," he said and laughed again. "Are you ready to go back now?" he asked me.

I shook my head. "No," I said.

"You'd better let him stay with me a spell," Hannah said, and her voice was soft again and I felt she wasn't mad at Big Eli for what he had done.

"Come home when you're a'mind," said Big Eli and snapped his fingers at Faro. They started down the path the way they had come and Hannah and I stood on the porch and watched them until they were lost in the timber. I wanted to run after them and tell Big Eli about the dream but I had chewed my cud and I knew I had to swallow it. We went back into the house and began clearing the dishes.

CHAPTER XXV

Moses was still scolding from the top of the sycamore and the potlicker was restless and growling when Hannah and I finished the dishes and I wondered if Big Eli had changed his mind and come back for me. I heard the potlicker whine and scuffle off the porch but she didn't bark. I hung the drying rag on the pot rack in the fireplace and when I turned around I saw a shadow in the square of sunlight that came through the kitchen door. I reached a hand out and touched Hannah and she wheeled and saw it too. Then Stan Bodine stood there with the potlicker beside him. Hannah let go a short scream.

Bodine's face was covered by a scraggly beard and his riggin' was wrinkled and dirty. He looked at the two of us, grinned and came in.

"I see you've got company," he said to Hannah, meaning me.

"Why did you come back?" she asked.

He only chuckled, husky and dry throated.

"They'll get you," she said.

"Ain't you aiming to kiss me?" he asked and moved a pace toward her, the grin spreading.

She moved to put the table betwix them. He stopped short.

"You didn't seem to mind Eli Wakefield's kissing you," he said and I knew he had seen it happen. She didn't try to deny it.

"Peekers get dust in their eyes," she said.

He looked at me. "What's this young'un doing here?" he asked her.

"You let him be," she said and her eyes flashed.

The vittles had not been taken off the table and he went to the sideboard where I had piled the dishes and got a plate and helped himself. She laid a knife and fork for him and poured a gourd of water which he gulped and she filled it again. While he ate he asked about the stock and she told him that the man who sold him the farm had taken the two horses, the rig and the cow for debt.

"You can sell the mules and the hogs tomorrow," he said. "I'll be needing the money before I go."

She looked scared. "You're not going to stay here, Stan," she said. "I've heard them prowling around at night looking for you."

"Looks like Eli Wakefield did most of the prowling since I've been gone," he said and laughed. "Maybe I'd better be on hand when he comes to get his young'un."

She didn't answer him. He shoved his chair back and Hannah started to pick up his plate when he grabbed her.

He stopped and glared at me. "Get out of here," he yelled at me, and I started for the door. "Wait!" he shouted and I stopped.

Hannah slid out of his arms.

"Don't go after your pappy," he said, "or I'll kill her."

I looked at Hannah to see what she wanted me to do.

"He means it, Little Eli," she said.

I went outside and I heard the door closed and the heavy bar dropped into place. I sat down on a chopping block in the back yard to think things over. I remembered seeing a pistol on the mantel over the kitchen fireplace and the rifle stacked next to the door and I wondered if they were loaded. The pistol was double barreled and fired by cap. The rifle fired by flint and would need powder in the pan. I decided that in case of trouble I'd stand the best chance of killing him with the pistol, though I had never fired one.

Moses flew down from the sycamore and begged for something to eat. I rolled the chopping block over and he scrambled for grubs and crickets. I heard the back door open again and Bodine stood staring at me, a Beelzebub grin on his face. I rolled another block over like I didn't see him and with my fingers I dug grubs out of the damp ground and tossed them to Moses. Bodine studied the crow for a spell then stepped into the yard and came toward me at a slow shuffle. Hannah came to the door and watched him like she was afraid of what he was going to do.

Moses backed off and scolded when he saw Bodine. Crows don't like strangers and he had never seen Bodine before.

Bodine settled himself on the chopping block, picked up a dry chip and began whittling on it with his pocketknife. It must have been the same knife he sunk in Bob Morgan's heart.

"When's your pappy coming back for you?" he asked.

"He's not coming back," I said.

"It won't do you no good to lie," he said. "I'll be waiting for him when he gets here."

Hannah came up to us. "He's telling the truth, Stan," she said. "Why don't you let him alone?"

Bodine paid her no heed, but his face reddened.

"Has your pappy been courtin' my woman?" he asked.

"No," I said, and Hannah said, "Stan Bodine, you shut up!"

He kicked over a block and crickets began jumping. Moses forgot his fear of Bodine and started catching them. Bodine watched him like he had never seen it happen before.

"How long's this critter been here?" he asked without taking his eyes off Moses.

"He's the boy's pet," Hannah said. "He brought him here a spell back."

"Thought he acted like he'd been here a spell," Bodine said and picked up another whittling chip. He was silent for a while and then he said, "I once knew a feller who had a talking crow." He rustled a chuckle. "I'll wager this critter would have a lot to say if he could talk. He could tell me a lot of things. Like how many times Eli Wakefield has been here to see my woman while I've been gone."

"I'll take the boy home," Hannah said and put her hand on my shoulder. "I'll take him home!"

"No you ain't," Bodine said and glared at her. "Nar one of you leave until I'm gone!" He tossed the chip to the ground and fingered the edge of his blade with a stubby thumb.

A cricket hop-skipped across the ground with Moses after him. The cricket hid under the toe of Bodine's boot and

Moses tried to peck him out. Bodine reached out a fat hand
and grabbed Moses by the neck and the crow beat his wings
and squalled to get free. It happened so quick I couldn't stop
him.

"Let him go!" I yelled and rushed at Bodine. He shoved me
aside with the hand that held the knife and began to laugh. I
tried to beat him with my fists but Hannah grabbed and held
me. She was afraid of that knife and what he would do with
it.

"There's only one way to make a crow talk," Bodine said,
"and that's to split his tongue." The thumb and forefinger
closed tight on Moses' throat and I saw the beak pop open as
he struggled for air.

Hannah screamed and held on to me tighter as I tried to
break free. Bodine's right hand moved quick with the knife
and blood spurted from Moses' mouth.

"You devil!" Hannah screamed. "You devil!"

Bodine threw back his head and laughed, then flung Moses
to the ground where he began to claw at his beak with his
foot, but no sound came from him. I managed to break
away from Hannah.

"I'll kill you!" I yelled at Bodine and ran for the kitchen
door. Hannah guessed what I was going to do for she ran
after me and Bodine was right behind her.

We both reached the fireplace at the same time but Hannah was taller and grabbed the pistol before I could lay hands
to it. I tried to get it from her but she held it high and all the
time saying, "No, Little Eli! No!"

"I'll brain you!" I heard Bodine bellow and turned to see
him pick up the rifle by the barrel. He came in swinging it
like a club. I ducked and the butt of the gun whizzed over my
head. Before he could swing again, Hannah shoved me aside
and pointed the pistol at Bodine.

"I'll shoot!" she said. There was killing in her eyes and in
her voice. Bodine stopped to study her and the soggy grin
came back again.

"I mean it, Bodine," she said. "I'll kill you if you touch
him!"

"That ain't loaded," he said. "You can't bluff me."

She lowered the muzzle. "Don't make me prove it," she said.

His eyes fixed on the pistol and he moved one step toward her. I looked at Hannah to see what she was going to do about it. I could see she was trying to make up her mind. Bodine took another step and the gun roared and my ears buzzed like a nest of hornets. A splinter from the table spun in the air and fell at Bodine's feet.

"There's a load in the other barrel," she said, and then asked, "Do you want it?"

"You wouldn't dare," he said and turned his back on her.

I saw a whiskey jug on the table. It hadn't been there before. Bodine got his hat and lifted a powder horn from a peg beside the fireplace. Then he came to the table, picked up the jug and with the rifle cupped in his arm he stalked out. When he cleared the door he stopped and turned around to look at us.

"Don't try leaving the house," he said. "I'll be watching if you do."

Then he was gone and I heard his footsteps fade across the back yard. Hannah shut the door and dropped the wooden bar into place. Then she went to the front door and did the same. She put the pistol back on the mantel over the kitchen fireplace and slumped in a chair by the table. Then she sank her head in her arms beside his dirty plate and cried.

CHAPTER XXVI

AFTER A SPELL I went to the window and looked out. Moses was crouched against the chopping block and he was still clawing at his beak and shaking his head. I knew he was bad hurt or he would be in the top of the sycamore. I lifted the cross bar from the door and Hannah jumped up and tried to stop me.

"He'll kill you!" she called to me but I got the door open and ran into the yard. Moses tried to get away from me but I picked him up.

"Hurry!" Hannah called from the kitchen door.

I raced into the kitchen and she slammed and barred the door behind me.

"He's gone," I said.

She shook her head. "No he's not," she said. "He's waiting out there somewhere. He thinks Big Eli will be back for you."

I put Moses on the hearth but he was too weak to stand and he sort of slumped over on one side with his wings spread out. He gasped for breath. She got an old shirt and we wrapped him up warm. Shortly after sundown Moses died and Hannah and I both cried a little.

"I wish I had shot him," she said, meaning Bodine, and sobbed on my shoulder.

"Somebody will," I said.

We didn't eat any supper that night and we didn't light a candle either. She said Bodine might try to shoot through a window and kill me. When the Seth Thomas clock struck ten she said we should get some sleep.

She brought a rocking chair in the kitchen and spread a bear hide over it. "I'll sleep here," she said, "and you can sleep in the bed." She went into the next room and I heard her turning down the quilts and fluffing the tick. When she came back I was in the rocking chair.

145

"I'd rather sleep here," I said, and I was glad that it was dark and she couldn't see my face and read my thoughts.

"If you fancy," she said. "If you hear anything, call me."

I said I would and she went in the next room. I heard her take off her shoes but when the rawhide thongs of the bedstead creaked under her weight I knew she was going to sleep with her clothes on. I took off my boots and let them clump loud on the hearth so she would hear them. I settled down in the bear hide but I knew I wasn't going to sleep. I wanted to think. Moses was laying dead on the hearth and Hannah and I were holed up in Stan Bodine's house like animals at bay and somewhere out there in the dark he was waiting with a muzzle-loader in case we tried to make a run for it. I could hear Hannah tossing about in her bed and after an hour I let on like I was snoring. It was soon after that her breathing got steady and she didn't move and I knew she was asleep at last.

I was certain I had seen a flicker of light through the kitchen window. I slipped out of the bear hide and prayed that a floorboard wouldn't give me away. I made it without noise and I was right about the light. I could see the faint glow of a smouldering fire three hundred yards or more from the house. Bodine, I knew, was drunk or he wouldn't have made a fire.

I went back to the rocking chair and watched the window until the light didn't flicker any more. The clock struck midnight and Hannah moved on the bed. I knew the potlicker wasn't on the front porch or anywhere near because I would have heard her scratching fleas. She was with Bodine, I knew, and Moses wouldn't be able to sound a warning. I stood on tiptoe and got the pistol and shoved it under my belt, then I went to the back door in my sock feet. It seemed it took an hour to lift the cross bar and open the door without making a noise but I did it. The night air was chilly and the heavy dew soaked through my socks, but it muffled the dry leaves when I got into the timber. I stopped to rest because my heart was pounding like a sledge. The fire had died down and I could hardly make out Bodine squatted against the base of a tree. The jug was between his feet. I couldn't see the potlicker at all.

I knew I would have to get closer and I began to inch my way forward, feeling ahead with my hands for twigs and dry leaves that might give me away. I judged I was fifty yards from him when I stopped again and lay flat on my belly until my breath steadied. I could see the potlicker then, curled up a yard from the coals with her back toward them. I could see the outline of a whiskey still too. Bodine's head bobbed in a doze. I drew the pistol from my belt and leveled it in a practice aim but I wasn't certain I could hit him at that distance because my hands were cold and shaking and I couldn't see the sights in the dark either.

Then I remembered that one barrel had been fired by Hannah and I slipped a thumb over the lock. Both hammers were down and I knew I'd have to cock them both before I could find out which barrel hadn't been fired. I eased back the hammers and they cocked with a click. The potlicker lifted her head and "wuffed" a low growl. Bodine sat up straight and turned his face toward the house and me. He listened and I held my breath.

After a few seconds he leaned back against the tree and I ran my thumb over the lock of the pistol. By feeling the caps I knew it was the right barrel that Hannah had fired. The left cap was smooth. I raised the gun to aim again, because I knew I couldn't get any closer without fretting the potlicker. I could see Bodine in the sights then, and I began to tighten my grip on the stock. Then, from far off somewhere, I seemed to hear Big Eli reciting Scripture like he used to before we came to The Purchase.

"Thou shalt not kill," his voice seemed to be saying over and over. I tried to shut my ears to it but I kept hearing him, "Thou shalt not kill." I tried to get Bodine in the sights again but my eyes were blurred. My hands began to shake and I was afraid my fingers would trip the trigger. I lowered the gun and laid it on the ground. I knew I couldn't do it.

Bodine reached over and chunked the fire and a small flame leaped up. A twig cracked somewhere and the potlicker woke up snarling. I saw Bodine ease his hand toward the muzzle-loader stacked against the tree and then I heard the roar of a gun and I saw the flash of it less than a hundred yards away. Bodine toppled forward on his face and lay still.

The potlicker snarled and dashed out of the rim of light and I heard a man crashing through the brush. I wondered if it was Big Eli. One thing was certain, whoever it was, neither he nor I could have got that close to Bodine if Moses had been alive. Bodine had plaited his own hang noose when he killed him.

Then I heard Hannah. "Eli! Eli!" she screamed as she ran toward me, guided by the dull glow of the fire. I picked up the pistol and went to where Bodine sprawled on the ground. When she got there she knelt over him and I helped her turn him over on his back. There was a big hole in his forehead and blood was oozing out of it. The potlicker was still barking and snarling a piece away. Hannah took the pistol out of my hand and without looking at it laid it on the ground next to Bodine's body.

"Why did you do it, Little Eli?" she said, "Why did you do it?"

Until I knew who killed him I didn't want her to know it wasn't me who did it, so I said, "He begged his own chaw and chawed more than he begged."

She looked at Bodine and shuddered. Then she said, "I've got to take you home, Little Eli."

We went back to the house and I put on my boots while she got a cape and lit a lantern. Then we went to the stable and saddled a mule. She helped me in the saddle and handed me the reins and then climbed up behind me, sitting sideways on his rump. We jogged off down the trail toward Humility and a whippoorwill wailed. Day would be breaking by the time we got there.

CHAPTER XXVII

NEITHER of us said much as we rode along. I was wondering who it was that killed Bodine. The more I thought about it the more certain I was that Big Eli or one of the Morgan men had done it. And yet I asked myself why should a Morgan run away after he did it? Big Eli would have a good reason. He wouldn't want Hannah to know he had killed her husband. He would have run to keep her from knowing he did it. But that would not have made any difference to Anse or Tully or Terry Morgan. They would have killed Stan Bodine and been proud to admit it even to her. They wouldn't have run. It must have been Big Eli, I decided, and if it was I didn't want Hannah to ever know it. I decided to stick to my story that I had shot Bodine. She already thought I did and she had good reasons for thinking so.

Breakfast smoke was rising from most of the chimneys in the village when we drew up in front of Uncle Zack's and slid off the mule. Faro didn't meet us and I wondered why. Uncle Zack heard us ride up and came to the door. His eyebrows popped up in surprise when he saw who it was.

"Come in," he said, and as we walked into the big room Aunt Soph came from the kitchen and she was so surprised to see Hannah that she almost dropped the skillet she held in her hand. They knew something was wrong.

"Where's Elias?" Uncle Zack said.

Before I could answer Aunt Soph said, "He's been gone the night. We thought he was looking for you."

Hannah said, "Squire, Bodine's been killed."

Aunt Soph started to cluck.

"Killed!" said Uncle Zack and stared at her. "Did Elias kill him?" he asked.

Hannah didn't answer but started to cry.

"I killed him," I said.

Aunt Soph clasped her hands and shut her eyes. "God have mercy," she said and she began to weep.

"Amen," said Uncle Zack. He went to the front door and looked up and down the road, then he said to Aunt Soph, "Fix them something to eat. I'll get Doc Haney and send for the Sheriff." He put on his hat and went out and Aunt Soph told us to come to the kitchen with her. While she fixed the vittles she kept looking side glances at Hannah and I knew she was wishing she could blame everything on her. Hannah kept crying and couldn't eat anything, but I was hungry and I wondered why I was. Twice in a short spell of my life I had seen men die before my eyes and both times it seemed to whet my appetite instead of dulling it. I couldn't understand it.

Before I was through eating, people started coming in the house and I knew that Uncle Zack had lost no time in spreading the news. They didn't ask any questions but stood around and stared at me and Hannah. Miss Susie Spann came in and Aunt Soph met her. They put their arms around each other and Aunt Soph busted out crying again and Miss Susie was glaring over Aunt Soph's shoulder at Hannah. When Aunt Soph let go of her she came over and before I could do anything about it she leaned down and kissed me. "God have mercy on you, Little Eli," she said and I wiped off the wet of her kiss with my sleeve.

Uncle Zack came back in a spell and Big Eli was with him. Folks made way for them as they came through the door. The Gabriel Horn was swinging from his shoulder and he stopped to hang it on the peg by the fireplace.

He came over and stood looking at me for a spell like he was trying to read my thoughts. I held back the tears.

"Who killed Bodine, Little Eli?" he asked.

"I shot him," I said.

He looked at Hannah. "Did he?" he asked.

Hannah choked a cry and nodded her head. "Yes," she said.

Big Eli took a deep breath and he set his mouth hard across his teeth. "You're a liar," he said, and then I was certain that he had done it himself.

Hannah looked up at him in wonderment and I knew she

couldn't understand why he would call her a liar. Her mouth
half opened like she was going to say something, but she
didn't. She just stared at him and I saw Aunt Soph and Miss
Susie Spann and the other women looking at each other like
they believed she killed Stan Bodine. I don't know what
would have happened but Doc Haney came in carrying his
little black bag of cures.

"Where's the body?" he asked Hannah and she told him.

He turned to Uncle Zack and Big Eli. "We won't wait for
the Sheriff," he said. "We'll go up there now."

Uncle Zack and Big Eli went to the stable to harness the
mules to the wagon and everybody else hurried out behind
them to get teams hitched too.

Doc Haney led the procession astride his fat bay mare.
Hannah and Big Eli and I rode with Uncle Zack in the wagon
while the mule we had come on trailed behind. Aunt Soph
and Miss Susie rode with the blacksmith and his wife and
other wagons and rigs followed them.

Nobody in our wagon said anything, but Hannah cried
most of the way and squeezed my hand until at times it hurt.
Once or twice I saw Big Eli looking at her like he wanted to
choke the truth out of her and make her say that I hadn't
done it. I wondered if he would tell Doc Haney and the
Sheriff that he had done it, now he thought she was trying to
put the blame on me. It gave me two reasons for sticking to
my story. I knew there had been talk about Hannah and Big
Eli coming to The Purchase together and about him going up
alone to her place the night Bodine killed Bob Morgan. I
didn't want people to think that he had killed Bodine because
of Hannah or that she had killed Bodine because of Big Eli.

When we got there everybody piled out of the wagons
and rigs and they followed along in a pack when Hannah
and I led them to where Stan Bodine lay by the ashes of his
fire. They stood in a circle about us while Doc Haney looked
at the hole in Bodine's forehead.

"Might as well hold the inquest now," Doc Haney said
and began picking out six men in the crowd as jurors. I knew
all of them. The first was the blacksmith and I recollected

that he was the one who spread the news about Hannah and Big Eli coming to The Purchase together. The third juror was the man whose tooth Big Eli had jerked out with his fingers. The tavern keeper was another and the other three were farmers. As they were taking the oath, Anse, Tully and Terry Morgan rode up horseback. All three were armed with pistols which stuck out of their belts. They nodded to Big Eli and when they looked at me, Anse smiled and winked. I knew what he meant. He thought I had killed Bodine and he was proud of me for doing it.

Doc Haney sat down on a stump. Bodine had cut the tree to make firewood for his still. "Let's take testimony," he said, and motioned for me to stand before him. "Hold up your right hand, Son," he said, and when I did he said the oath and I said, "I do," and yet I knew I was going to lie with almost every breath I took.

"Why were you up here at Bodine's place?" he asked me. I hadn't thought he would ask that and I looked at Big Eli, but I didn't answer.

"Speak up, Son," said Doc. "Why were you up here last night?"

I shook my head. "I won't tell you," I said.

Doc spat on the ground and cleared his throat. "Then tell what you want to tell, Son," he said.

I began at the part where Bodine sneaked in while Hannah and I were clearing the dishes. I told about Bodine's splitting Moses' tongue with his pocketknife and how I had run into the house to get the pistol to kill him but Hannah took it away from me. I didn't leave out anything except the part about seeing somebody else shoot Bodine.

"That'll be all, Son," said Doc and motioned for Hannah to hold up her right hand. He said the oath and she said, "I do."

"Tell us what happened," Doc said.

She told it just like I had done, only she put in the part where Big Eli had come after me and she had asked that he let me stay. I thought Aunt Soph's eyes would pop out when she heard that and she started clucking and patting her toe in the dirt. Miss Susie never looked at Big Eli when she heard it but she didn't take her eyes off of Hannah. I wondered what she was thinking.

Big Eli reached down and picked up the pistol and began looking at it like he wasn't interested in what Hannah was saying, or what Doc Haney was asking her.

When she told all there was to tell, including the part where she found me standing over Bodine with the pistol in my hand, Doc Haney asked her, "When did you marry Bodine?"

"The second night after I got to The Purchase," she said.

"Had you know'd him before?" Doc asked. She shook her head. "No," she said.

"That was mighty quick courtin', wasn't it?" Doc asked.

"I was scared they'd take me back to Cadiz," she said, "and Bodine said they couldn't if I'd marry him."

Doc Haney asked her to explain what she meant and she told how she had run away from Cadiz with Big Eli and me and how the innkeeper and a constable had come for her and she ran away from Uncle Zack's too.

"I hid all night in the woods," she said, "and the next day I started walking. I got as far as Bodine's place here. He took me in and fed me and he must have known something was wrong, but I didn't tell him what happened. He said I could stay in the house that night as he had to go to Wadesboro anyway. He left, but around midnight he got back and he had a preacher with him. He told me the constable and the innkeeper were still looking for me and they'd take me back unless I married him. I was scared and said I would if he'd promise to pay off the indenture. He promised. Then the preacher wed us."

I looked at Big Eli and he was still fingering the pistol like he wasn't listening.

"Any witnesses to that wedding?" Doc Haney asked.

She didn't answer right off but looked like she was surprised. "No," she finally said, "there was nobody but Bodine and me and the preacher."

"What preacher was it?" Doc Haney asked.

"Bodine called him Zybee Fletcher," she said.

If somebody had hit me with a ham hock I wouldn't have been more surprised. Men began laughing and the women chattered and giggled like a bunch of jaybirds. Hannah looked at me and I thought she was going to start crying. Doc Haney yelled for order but he had to yell twice before things quieted down. Then he shook his head and looked at Hannah like he was sorry for her.

"Girl," he said, "you wasn't wed to Stan Bodine."

"But I was," she said. "I wouldn't lie to you."

"I know you wouldn't," said Doc, and he meant it. "But Zybee Fletcher ain't no preacher. He's a snake doctor."

The laughing started again. Everybody knew Zybee Fletcher, the snake doctor, and how he had told Big Eli that the King would buy our pearls. It was a lowdown trick, but he and Stan Bodine had pulled a meaner one on Hannah. Even Doc Haney was laughing, but I didn't think it was funny and neither did Big Eli, for his face got glazing red. All of a sudden he stood up and folks saw him and how mad he was and things quieted quick, for he was holding the pistol in his hand.

"Somebody's lying here, Doc," he said, and poked the pistol toward the coroner.

Doc Haney looked at the gun, saw it was butt first.

"Look at that gun," said Big Eli.

Doc did. "What about it?" he asked.

I knew then that Big Eli had caught up on the lie I had told about killing Bodine myself.

"According to their testimony," Big Eli said, "this gun was fired twice. Once by her and once by my son, Eli."

"Yes," said Doc, "that's the testimony."

"Then how is it that one barrel is still loaded?" asked Big Eli and he glared at Hannah.

Doc looked close at the pistol, then he turned to Hannah again. "Was this pistol reloaded after you fired it in the table?" he asked.

"No," she said, "and Bodine took the powder horn with him when he left the house. It couldn't have been reloaded."

Everybody was craning their necks to hear what she said

and trying to get a look at the gun. Doc Haney shooed them back to get breathing space.

"I knew my boy didn't kill him," Big Eli said.

"Then who do you think did?" asked the coroner.

"She did, and Little Eli is lying to protect her," he said. Hannah made a little scream and clasped her hands together.

I could hardly believe what I heard. I knew Big Eli had killed him and I couldn't believe he would blame it on her. At that second I hated him as bad as I had hated Bodine.

"That's a lie!" I yelled. "She didn't do it! You did it!"

I picked up a chunk from the dead fire and threw at him.

Bedlam broke loose and the coroner and Uncle Zack started yelling for order. Hannah grabbed me and held me close to her. Big Eli tried to take me away and I kicked him and spit on him. "You did it!" I shouted. "You killed him!"

When things quieted down, Doc Haney put his hand on my shoulder and said, "Son, you swore to tell the truth. Now let's have it."

I admitted I lied. I told how I had gone down to the campfire aiming to kill Bodine but I couldn't make myself do it. I told of hearing the gunshot and seeing the flash of it less than a hundred yards from me. I told of hearing a man run away.

"I didn't see him," I said, "but I knew all the time it was Big Eli." I broke out crying when I saw Big Eli looking at me like he was positive I was still lying.

Doc Haney was looking at Big Eli too. He spat on the ground, then asked, "Where were you after midnight, Wakefield?"

"Hunting," said Big Eli.

"Got witnesses to prove it?" Doc asked.

"No," said Big Eli.

I heard horses trotting up and saw Sheriff Conse Foster and Miss Susie Spann's brother, Jim. Nobody paid any attention as they dismounted and pushed through the crowd.

"You've been friendly with this girl, haven't you," Doc asked, nodding his head toward Hannah.

Before Big Eli could answer the Sheriff looked around sort of perplexed. "What're you holding a hearing for, Doc?" he asked.

"To find out who killed Stan Bodine and why," said Doc.

"You're wasting time and breath," said the Sheriff, and he pointed at Miss Susie's brother. "Jim Spann killed him."

That knocked the wind out of everybody, including me. All we did was stare at Miss Susie's brother while he stood looking at the hole in Stan Bodine's head and the dried blood on the dead face and the matted hair. It was the first chance he had of seeing his handiwork and he didn't look like he was enjoying it, for his skin turned persimmon yellow.

"Why did he kill him?" Doc Haney asked the Sheriff.

"For the bounty," said the Sheriff.

Nobody said a word but all looked at Jim Spann. He shifted from one foot to the other like he was standing on a hot coal.

I wondered how he could kill a man for money, even a man like Stan Bodine. I had meant to kill Bodine and though I had a reason, I couldn't do it. Big Eli should have killed him that day they had the fight, but he didn't do it. Hannah could have killed him with reason but she fired into the kitchen table instead. But none of us would have done it for money. Folks backed away from Jim Spann. Doc Haney spat in the dust and said in a voice that seemed weary and tired, "Raise your right hand, Spann." The hand was trembling when he stuck it up. Doc mumbled the oath and started taking testimony.

CHAPTER XXVIII

Aunt Soph motioned for me to come to her but Miss Susie Spann was standing next to her and I made out I didn't see. I went to Hannah instead and we listened to Jim Spann's testimony. He told how he had gone to Bodine's place several nights, hoping to catch him, but the dog had heard him and run him off. That's who Hannah had heard prowling about.

"How come the dog didn't hear you last night?" Doc Haney asked him.

"I don't know," Spann said.

I knew why. Bodine had killed Moses and Moses couldn't warn the potlicker.

After a few more questions Doc closed the case. The six jurors walked off a few paces into the woods and soon they came back with the verdict. The blacksmith said, "Deceased died from gunshot wound inflicted by one Jim Spann. Motive, bounty."

Doc Haney looked at the Sheriff. "You can pay the bounty, Sheriff." He got up and stretched his legs.

The women moved off toward the wagons and rigs. The men looked at each other, wondering what to do about Bodine's dead body. Big Eli came to Hannah.

"Where do you want him buried?" he asked her.

"He's got kin in the next county," she said. "I'll carry him there."

"You'd better get ready to travel," he said. "We'll take care of things here." He turned back to the men, and Hannah and I went back to the house.

She went inside to change her dress, but I followed her into the kitchen. Moses was on the hearth where he had died.

I picked him up and went outside and got a spade. The men were already sawing boards they had knocked off the stable shed to make a coffin for Stan Bodine. I dug a deep hole under the sycamore and dropped Moses in it, then raked the dirt over him and tapped it firm with my foot. When I got to the back yard, the Sheriff was waiting at the door and I could hear the blacksmith's wife talking to Hannah.

"Get a bucket of water," the Sheriff said to me. "We've got to scrub and shave him."

I got a washbowl from the kitchen and drew a bucket of water. The blacksmith's wife came out with a man's riggin', clean and smelling of soap, and handed them to the Sheriff.

"She says you can burn what he had on," she said to the Sheriff and he nodded that he would.

"Bring the bucket, Son," he said and I followed him.

Doc Haney was sitting on the stump when we got back to the body. He opened his pill case and brought out a razor and whetted it on the calf of his boot. The Sheriff began washing the dried blood off Bodine's face. When he was through Doc Haney squatted down beside Bodine. He didn't bother to lather the stubble which was long and starting to curl. The razor made a rattling sound as it cut through the whiskers. Meanwhile the Sheriff was spreading a horse blanket on the ground. When Doc Haney finished shaving Bodine, he and the Sheriff lifted him, stiff as a paling, onto the blanket. Together they took off his clothes.

There was a long scar across the belly and Doc Haney pointed to it. "Them's my stitches, Sheriff," he said.

The Sheriff said, "He killed the feller who cut 'im, as I recollect," and Doc Haney nodded.

"Yes he did," Doc said. "When I sewed him up, I told him it was a waste of time. I knew somebody would kill him sooner or later."

By the time they got Bodine dressed in his clean riggin', Big Eli and Uncle Zack and some of the other men came down with the new-made coffin. They lifted Bodine into it and covered him with the horse blanket. The Sheriff dropped the rifle in beside the body and the men nailed on the lid. The Sheriff piled the bloody clothes where Bodine fell. He kicked leaves and dried sticks around them and then struck a match on his bootheel. The sulphur smell from the match made me feel sick when it mixed with the burning clothes.

All hands lifted the coffin and we started up the rise. Bodine's wagon with his two mules hitched to it was waiting in
front of the house and they put the coffin in it. Aunt Soph
and Miss Susie and the other women were standing off a few
paces looking on but saying nothing. Miss Susie's brother was
in the saddle, waiting to leave. With the coffin ready to go,
nobody seemed to know what to do next.

"I'll stay and see she gets off," Big Eli said to Uncle Zack
and the other men. "Little Eli will be with me."

That satisfied everybody. The men joined their women
and they began climbing in their rigs and wagons and on
horses. Uncle Zack's wagon moved off and the others followed.

The women kept glancing back until they rode into the
deep timber and I knew they had hoped to catch sight of
Hannah when she came out. When the sound of the last
wagon had faded out she came on the porch, carrying the
same carpetbag she had brought that night from Cadiz. She
was wearing a plain grey dress and a blue cape that almost
touched the floor, and she had covered her small hat with a
veil which was knotted under her chin, but through it I could
see that her eyes were red and swollen. Big Eli picked up the
bag.

"I'm sorry for what I said," he said to her, holding his hat
in his free hand.

"I hold no vex," she said.

"You shouldn't go alone," he said. "We'll ride along, if
you pleasure."

She shook her head. "His kin knows you put up bounty,"
she said. "I know the way."

"What about the stock here?" he asked.

"Turn them out to forage," she said, and stepped into the
yard. We followed her to the wagon. Big Eli dropped the
bag beside the coffin and began unwinding the reins from
the whipstock. Hannah bent down and hugged and kissed me.

"I'm glad you didn't kill him," she said, and her lips trem-
bled. Then she stood up straight again and Big Eli took her
hand and histed her into the wagon seat. He handed her the

The Sheriff shoved back his chair and left. Big Eli sat down and put the jug on the table beside him. The man in the fancy riggin' pulled up a chair for me.

"Obliged," I said like Big Eli had taught me.

The man smiled at me and then he asked Big Eli, "Was this my bed pardner the other night?"

Everybody laughed.

"Yes," said Big Eli, and he turned to me. "Little Eli," he said, "this is the man from Texas."

"Did you think a grizzly was in bed with you?" the man asked and laughed, but he patted me on the shoulder.

I felt my face turning hot red. He and everybody else knew about my running away but none of them, I was glad, knew why I had done it. I wasn't going to tell, so I didn't answer.

The man from Texas stuck out his hand and we shook.

"Babson's my name," he said. "Pleasant Tuesday Babson is the whole of it."

I thought he was topping cotton. "Mighty strange name," I said and grinned.

"Not so strange when you know how I come by it," he said.

He didn't wait for me to ask how he did.

"The way my mammy told it, God rest her soul, when she came to after the pain and rigor of bornin' me, she looked up from the ground where she was laying and she saw the bright sun in the sky and heard the birds singing in the trees and smelled the sweet breath of Godamighty's flowers on the June air," he went on. "My pappy put me in her arms to suck at her boosom and she asked him, 'What day is this?' and he told her it was of a Tuesday. 'That's what we'll name him,' she told my pappy. 'We'll name him Pleasant Tuesday.' So, Son, that's what it's been ever since. Pleasant Tuesday Babson."

He chuckled. "Not so strange a name now is it, Son?" he asked.

"It's a good name," I said, and I knew I liked the man from Texas.

The Sheriff came back with Jim Spann trailing at his heels and looking like a sheep-killing dog. Everybody was quiet and Spann looked at the faces about the table and I knew he wished they wasn't there, but he didn't say anything.

"Draw up a chair," said Big Eli. The Sheriff shoved one under Spann and pressed him into it, then sat down himself. Big Eli turned to the bar and called, "Bring glasses for four."

He reached in his pocket and brought out the bounty. He piled it in front of him and when the glasses were brought he unstoppered the jug and began to fill them. Spann reached out a hand. "Pass me up," he said. "I seldom imbibe."

Big Eli filled the glass and shoved it in front of him.

"Just a toast," he said, his voice calm but his eyes dark as a storm cloud. "Pick it up."

Spann's eyes wandered to the money on the table and back to Big Eli. He picked up the glass and raised it in front of him. Big Eli, the Sheriff and the man from Texas did too.

"Here's to Stan Bodine who's on his way to hell with a hole in his head," said Big Eli, and he let the grog slide betwix his lips. The Sheriff and Pleasant Tuesday Babson swallowed theirs and Spann tried to toss his off fast. It must have tasted like lye for he shut his eyes, gulped and began to cough. Big Eli pounded him on the back, but nobody laughed. Big Eli filled the glasses again and Spann, who was breathing so hard he couldn't say anything, shook his head that he didn't want any more. Big Eli made like he didn't see him. He looked at Pleasant Tuesday.

"Pleasant Tuesday," he said, "what do you reckon old Beelzebub will say to Stan Bodine when he shows up in hell with a hole in his head?"

Pleasant Tuesday thought a spell. "Why, I reckon Beelzebub will ask him how he come by it," he said, and picked up his glass of grog.

The Sheriff spun his glass betwixt thumb and forefinger and his pale watery eyes narrowed into a cold smile.

"What do you reckon Stan Bodine will tell Beelzebub?" Big Eli went on.

"What will he tell him?" said Pleasant Tuesday.

"Bodine will say to Beelzebub," said Big Eli, "Beelzebub, I don't know how I come by this hole in my head. I was bushwhacked."

The faces about the table began to grin, and Jim Spann laughed but I knew he wasn't enjoying himself.

"Let's drink to Beelzebub," Big Eli said and lifted his grog. "Drink to Beelzebub, Spann," he said.

Spann lifted his glass and looked at the Sheriff and Pleasant Tuesday. They all gulped and Spann choked again. Big Eli pounded him on the back to where I thought he would split his spine. Then he began counting out the money, but he didn't shove it across the table to Spann. When he was through he poured another round.

"Another toast," he said.

"I don't want any more," said Spann.

"You want this bounty, don't you?" Big Eli asked.

Spann didn't answer but picked up the glass.

"Here's to the bushwhacker who sent Stan Bodine to hell with a hole in his head," said Big Eli. He gulped his grog and so did the Sheriff and Pleasant Tuesday.

Spann put his glass down without drinking it. He reached across the table for the bounty but Big Eli brought the jug down on his fingers.

"One more toast," Big Eli said, and filled the three empty glasses.

"I won't drink it," Spann said. Big Eli paid him no heed.

"Don't you like this grog?" Big Eli asked, looking at him like he was surprised.

"I don't like grog," said Spann.

Big Eli raised his glass. So did Pleasant Tuesday Babson and the Sheriff.

"Here's to the bounty," Big Eli said. "May it be as bitter as Bodine's booze." He gulped the grog and so did the Sheriff and Pleasant Tuesday. He shoved the bounty across the table and Jim Spann raked it in. Spann shoved it into his jeans and pushed back his chair. As he did Big Eli picked up the glass of grog that Spann had not touched. With a flick of his wrist he threw the grog in Spann's face. Spann paid him no heed but headed for the door and we watched as he left. There was a rustle of boots on the floor.

Big Eli looked at the men about us. "Anybody else want a drink of Bodine's grog?" he asked, and nobody did. He stood up and swung the jug with all his might at the stone fireplace. It crashed into pieces and the grog ran over the hearth and onto the floor.

"Come on, Little Eli," he said, and we left the tavern.

CHAPTER XXX

UNCLE ZACK AND AUNT SOPH were as glum as possums up a sour 'simmon tree when we got back, but they were thinking plenty about what had happened and I knew it would ooze out like fester from a boil sooner or later. Both looked at Big Eli and sniffed the air to make certain he wasn't drunk, which he wasn't. After a while Uncle Zack said, "You were a fool to put up so much bounty, Elias."

"It was my money," said Big Eli, "and it was worth it to get shed of one polecat and see the stripes of another."

Uncle Zack shook his head. "There's folks who'll agree with you, I reckon," he said.

"It's not like Bodine had put up a fight and had to be killed," Big Eli said, "but bushwhacking for bounty is mighty lowdown."

Uncle Zack agreed. "I'm mighty glad it wasn't you who killed him," Aunt Soph said.

"I had plenty of reason," said Big Eli. "And so did the Morgans, and if Little Eli had done it, like he claimed, he had reason too I reckon."

I could tell by the way Uncle Zack and Aunt Soph looked at each other that they didn't agree with him, but they kept their thoughts to themselves. Aunt Soph got supper and when we sat down to eat, Uncle Zack said a blessing. It had to do with the blessedness of a pure heart and heavenly rewards of turning away wrath.

Big Eli looked at him when he finished. "Just who were you praying for, Zack?" he asked.

Uncle Zack's face got red and he didn't answer until he had filled his plate.

"It's not right to have murder in the heart," he said. "Scripture tells us it is a sin." He looked at me. "And yet," he said, "there was murder in the heart of this boy last night. He said so himself. He told Doc Haney that he went down there to kill Stan Bodine for what he had done to him. He wasn't willing to turn away wrath. He wanted to do murder."

He took a mouthful, chewed and swallowed it.

"But Little Eli is but a child, and he couldn't reason like a grownup, so somebody had to reason for him. There he lay in the leaves with a loaded pistol pointed at Stan Bodine. His finger was on the trigger and there was hate and murder in his heart. Hate told him to pull the trigger. Then something happened to this boy. Godamighty looked down and saw the loaded pistol in the hand of Little Eli. He saw the hate in his heart. And he saw the finger on the trigger. But Godamighty saw no reason in the mind of the child, he didn't. So he made a miracle and tore out the wrath in the boy's heart and he withered the finger that was trembling on the trigger. Withered it of the strength it took to pull it."

Uncle Zack went back to eating, and Big Eli looked at me. "How about it, Little Eli?" he asked.

I remembered how I had thought of the Scripture, "Thou shalt not kill," and I reckoned it meant the same thing Uncle Zack was talking about, but not so windy. "I reckon," I said.

"Amen," said Big Eli, and we all ate our supper.

That night Uncle Zack said, "Elias, I want to talk to you."

"Go ahead, Zack," said Big Eli.

"It's about Little Eli," Aunt Soph said, looking down her chubby nose at me. "There's going to be talk about you leaving him yonder with that sinful female."

"She's not sinful," I said, getting mad. I saw Big Eli's face pink up too.

"She didn't know she wasn't wed to Bodine," he said.

"Mebby so," Aunt Soph said, but I could tell by the way she said it she didn't believe her own words. "You've done the best you could for him, Elias, but God never aimed for man to raise young'uns like him."

"I'm pledged," said Big Eli.

"Folks would like it a heap if you'd set the date," said Uncle Zack.

"The lady sets the date, according to custom," said Big Eli. By the tone of his voice I knew he didn't like to have Uncle Zack and Aunt Soph pushing him.

He got up and reached for his hat. "Let's take a walk, Little Eli," he said. I wondered if he was turning away wrath, or running from it. I got my hat and we left.

CHAPTER XXXI

TORCHES of fat pine were burning in front of the tavern and as we got near I could see a crowd of men standing around listening to somebody talk. It was Pleasant Tuesday Babson. Big Eli and I edged in to listen too.

"It's Spanish country," he was saying. "It's not like country you ever saw before. You don't measure it by rod and chain in Texas. You measure it by the eye, and as far as the eye can see, and when your eye can see no farther there's where you drive your stakes."

Pleasant Tuesday then told how a man named Moses Austin rode into Texas on a mule with a black slave following him on foot.

"He rode right up to the Governor's palace," he said, "and asked for a grant of land to start a colony of Americans. The Governor listened to Moses Austin and knew him to be a wise man of great vision and he rewarded him with what he wanted. He gave him a tract of land so big it can only be spanned by the hand of God. Today, men and women just like you folks, are moving into Texas behind old Moses Austin just as the children of Israel followed the first Moses into the Promised Land."

Then Pleasant Tuesday told why he had come to Humility. He was getting up a party to journey to Texas and join Moses Austin's colony. He said the party would go by steamboat to New Orleans and from there by wagons and horseback to Texas.

"There's no wilderness to clear before a plowshare can be shoved into Texas ground," he said, "and the rifle ball's not been made that can carry to a neighbor's line."

He told about the abundance of game and when he said, "Mine own eyes have watched a sea of buffalo take from sunup to sundown to pass," people looked at each other like they thought Pleasant Tuesday might be topping cotton and they didn't believe him.

"Moses Austin died right after he set up his colony," Pleasant Tuesday said, "but his spirit leads on through his son. Godfearing men and women, who are brave of heart, will find a welcome in Texas."

After he got through talking, people crowded around him and asked questions. Big Eli and I stayed until it was past bedtime for Uncle Zack and Aunt Soph and then we went home. I couldn't go smack to sleep, because so many things had happened and I kept thinking about them. Big Eli must have been thinking about them too because he kept threshing around like a shoat in a sack long after he shucked his riggin' and climbed into bed.

I thought when things quieted down we would start work on our house again, but we didn't. Big Eli wasn't in the mind for it. For two days we roamed through the timber-covered hills and hunted. It was like it had been before we came to The Purchase, only Big Eli didn't sing when we built a fire and camped for the night. Big Eli shot only such game as the two of us needed to eat, and at night we listened to Faro run foxes through the draws and in the cane brakes along the river. It was the second night that Faro flushed a deer and I reckon he would have ended up in Tennessee if Big Eli hadn't blowed him in with the Gabriel Horn. It was a sharp blow and it stopped Faro's bay like his windpipe had been cut with a knife. And then Big Eli did something he hadn't done since we came to The Purchase.

He got down on his knees by the fire and prayed. I bowed my head and listened.

"Oh God give me wisdom," he prayed, "that I may do Thy will. Shed Thy good light on my troubled path that I may not stray into the byways of fools and, like a steer in a swamp, bog down in the quagmire of my own folly."

I knew what he meant. I had seen a steer get scared at the sight of us and plunge into a swamp and bog down and the more he threshed around to free himself the deeper he sank in the mire. Big Eli shot him to put him out of his misery. Big

Eli's prayer meant that he was afraid. He had never been afraid of anything before, and I wondered what it was. It made me afraid too.

He said "Amen," chunked up the fire and we crawled under the bear hide and we went to sleep. The next morning we headed back to Uncle Zack's. The sun was bright and beams of light broke through the leafy overhead and seemed always to stay just ahead of us. I wondered if it was God guiding our footsteps along a troubled path, and where He would lead us.

Aunt Soph and Uncle Zack saw us coming and they were mighty solemn of face when we walked in. Aunt Soph put her fingers to her lips and pointed to the closed door that opened into their bedroom. I knew she wanted us to be quiet.

"Miss Susie," she whispered. "She's asleep."

Big Eli looked at her in wonderment and Uncle Zack motioned for us to follow them into the kitchen. We did and he shut the door to the big room. We sat down about the kitchen table.

"She had trouble with her brother," said Aunt Soph in a low voice. "She had no other place to go, except here."

"What was the trouble betwixt them?" Big Eli asked.

"The bounty," Uncle Zack said.

"She told him it was a sin to kill a man for bounty," Aunt Soph said. "Even Bodine."

"He told her it was no worse to earn a bounty than to offer one," said Uncle Zack. "He meant you, Elias."

"I reckon," Big Eli said. "I had trouble with him at the tavern."

Uncle Zack nodded. "I hear," he said.

"She'll tell you about it, I reckon," Aunt Soph said.

About an hour later Miss Susie got up. She tried to be pleasant when she saw us and Uncle Zack tried to help her out.

"The bay window came yesterday," he said. "It's just the kind Miss Susie likes, isn't it, Miss Susie?"

Miss Susie said it was. Her eyes were red and I knew she had been crying. In my mind's eye, I couldn't see Miss Susie crying. She was the kind of woman who could smile but not laugh. She could frown but not scold, so I never knew for certain what she thought. It wasn't like her to weep.

Aunt Soph and Uncle Zack got busy with house chores and sent me to the store on an errand. That left Miss Susie and Big Eli by themselves in the kitchen. I don't know what they talked about. That afternoon Big Eli and Uncle Zack loaded the bay window glass in the wagon and the three of us drove to our house and put it in the frame. Uncle Zack stood in the big room and looked at the river through the window and the place where he was going to build a boat landing and freight sheds. Big Eli didn't have much to say.

We ate supper at home but Big Eli and I stayed in the tavern that night, for Miss Susie was sleeping in Aunt Soph's bed and Aunt Soph and Uncle Zack slept in our bed. The next morning, Big Eli saddled a mule and pulled me up behind him and we started for the new house again. We rode for a mile out of the village and then he swung the mule off the trail. He didn't say why and I wondered where he was going, but by the time we had gone another mile I knew we were heading for Stan Bodine's place.

The house was closed up but as we rode into the yard a man came out of the stables. Big Eli slipped me to the ground and he climbed out of the saddle. The man was a farmer who sold tobacco to Uncle Zack. He and Big Eli howdied but Big Eli didn't ask about Hannah. He talked about the weather, the price of tobacco and about new folks crowding in The Purchase. Finally he ran out of talk and the farmer asked him, "You looking for Bodine's woman?"

Big Eli admitted he was.

"She got back day before yesterday," he said, "and I was waiting with the mortgage. Bodine owed me. I made a settlement with her and she left afoot."

"Where did she go?" Big Eli asked.

"Couldn't get nothing out of her at all," said the farmer.

"Which way did she go?" asked Big Eli.

The farmer shook his head. "I was at the stables unhitching the team," he said. "I paid no heed."

Big Eli stood silent for a spell then he climbed in the saddle and pulled me up behind him and we started back the way we had come.

We went to the new house and that afternoon we put up two doors and chinked the fireplace. After supper that night Aunt Soph and Uncle Zack decided they should pay a call on the blacksmith and his wife. They took me along, leaving Big Eli and Miss Susie alone. It was almost midnight when Big Eli dropped by and got me and we went to sleep at the tavern. The next day we went to work on the new house again. While we worked, Faro chased rabbits until he tuckered out and came in to pant in the shade of a tulip tree. The sun was noon high and we were about to knock off and eat the snack Aunt Soph had fixed for us when I saw a man riding up the trail on a mule. Big Eli howdied him and asked if he wouldn't share our vittles, but the man said he reckoned he wasn't hungry. He slid to the ground and looked at Faro.

"Good dog, you've got," he said.

Big Eli agreed.

"I've heard of him of a night," the man said, meaning he had listened to Faro run foxes.

Big Eli didn't say anything and the man squatted on his hunkers and snapped his finger at Faro. "Let's take a look at you, dog," he said.

Big Eli stanced him and the man went over Faro with his hands, feeling the loose mouth and the broad chest. He turned to Big Eli and asked, "How much would you take for him?"

"What's your bid?" Big Eli asked and I couldn't believe I had heard him right.

The man named a price.

"Fair enough," said Big Eli, and the man reached into his jeans. Big Eli saw him and said, "But not today."

The man looked puzzled. "When?" he asked.

"I won't have need for him after Saturday week," he told the man. "You can get him then."

That satisfied the man and he climbed on his mule and rode off. Big Eli laid out the vittles, but he didn't touch them.

"Pitch in," he said to me.

I shook my head. "I'm not hungry," I said and walked away

because tears were coming to my eyes. I couldn't remember the time when we hadn't had Faro. I had often wondered how it would be when he got old and died, but I had never thought that someday Big Eli might sell him. But I knew why he was doing it now. Miss Susie Spann didn't like hunting men.

That night at supper, Miss Susie looked at me and smiled. "Little Eli," she said, "do you want to know a secret?"

"I know it already," I said.

She looked surprised.

"Big Eli and you get wed, come Sunday week," I said.

She looked at Big Eli, her eyes wide. "Did he tell you?" she asked.

"No," I said. "But he told the man to come for Faro on Saturday."

CHAPTER XXXII

UNCLE ZACK AND AUNT SOPH didn't lose any time spreading the news. Everywhere Big Eli went folks shook his hand and told him what a good woman he was getting. Aunt Soph and the blacksmith's wife got busy helping Miss Susie sew her wedding finery and Uncle Zack told Big Eli he would have to buy a ring. I wondered how much money Big Eli had left after paying the bounty but it must have been enough, for one morning he hitched two of Uncle Zack's horses to the rig and he and I started off bright and early for Paris, down in Tennessee.

It had rained and wagons had cut up the road and the going was bad. Sometimes I thought the team would bust the singletree they had to pull so hard through the mire.

"There's another road east of here," Big Eli said, "and we'll try it on the way back."

I remembered he had been to Paris before. That was the time he left Uncle Zack's for two days when he learned that Stan Bodine had wed Hannah Bolen.

Big Eli didn't waste much time buying the ring and we started back, but that road was as bad as the first one.

"There'll be a full moon tonight," he told me. "We'll stop and rest the horses and get a snack for ourselves."

"Where'll we stop?" I asked him.

"There's a road tavern down a piece," he said. "I stopped there when I rode this way before."

It was dark when we pulled up at the hitch rack in front of the tavern, and there were lots of horses and wagons around and I could hear loud laughing inside the tavern.

We went inside. The place was full of men, drinking and singing, and two men, so drunk they could scarce stand up were having a fight. The tavern keeper was trying to separate them but everybody else was trying to keep the fight going. It was funny because nobody was getting hurt and now and then the two fighters would turn on the tavern keeper and try to whip him. Big Eli and I sat down at a table to watch. That's why we didn't see her come up to our table and the first I knew she was there was when I heard her say, "I see she hasn't cut your hair yet," and she laughed.

Big Eli wheeled in his chair. "Hannah!" he said.

Then I saw that her lips and her cheeks were rosy red like the French women I had seen on the steamboat. I couldn't see her freckles at all.

"Been to buy the wedding ring?" she asked, and I wondered how she knew.

Big Eli didn't answer, but just looked at her.

"I hear lots of things from folks passing through," she said, and her speech was slow and heavy.

The tavern keeper had stopped the fight by then and things had quieted down some. Hannah smiled at me and ruffled my hair. "Don't let her shear your locks, Little Eli," she said and laughed and I saw her sway on her feet.

"I hate her," I said.

Hannah bent down like she was going to kiss me and she almost fell. Big Eli steadied her with his hand and she slapped it away.

Some of the men saw her push Big Eli's hand away and they moved toward us. Hannah threw back her head and began to laugh, a wild sort of laugh I had never heard from her before.

"I told you," she said to Big Eli, "that someday that woman would put a ring in your nose so you wouldn't stray. You bought the ring yourself. Come Sunday you'll put it on her finger, but come Monday she'll put it in your nose and it'll stay there for the rest of your life." She laughed and swayed against the table.

The men were glaring at Big Eli, like he had done something to Hannah. He got up from his chair.

"Come on," he said to me, and I got up too.

Some of the men started to block our way and I wondered what Big Eli would do to them. Hannah was laughing that wild laugh again.

"Let him go!" she said. "His woman's waiting for him!"

The men made a path for us and stood watching as we walked past and out the door to the team.

The moon was out and the team had no trouble following the road but neither of us said a word as we rocked in the rig toward Uncle Zack's. I knew that Big Eli was still traveling a troubled path.

CHAPTER XXXIII

AT BREAKFAST, Big Eli showed the ring to Uncle Zack and Aunt Soph and Uncle Zack began rubbing it on his coat sleeve.

"Pure gold," said Big Eli. "It won't rub off."

During the rest of the week Big Eli and I worked at the new house by day and he spent much time of an evening walking in the woods with Miss Susie. Aunt Soph's cupboard was getting filled with cakes and pies that she had cooked for the wedding party. Uncle Zack bought a keg of wine that had foreign words burned in the wood with a hot iron. He said they were French and that the wine had come from New Orleans but had been made in France fifty years before I was born.

Saturday morning they let me sleep late. After I had my breakfast I scraped up some scraps and went to the back door and called Faro, but he didn't come. I looked at Big Eli.

"The man came for him early," he said, and I knew Faro was gone.

Big Eli got his hat and went to the stables and saddled the mule. He left him standing in the yard and came into the house and got the rifle and the Gabriel Horn. "Let's go," he said to me.

He climbed in the saddle and pulled me up behind him and with the rifle across the pommel of the saddle we jogged off down the road for our last day of work on the new house. We spent the morning doing odd jobs that had been left to the last, such as putting up pegs to hang things on and making a bunk for me in the attic. Two of the pegs he put over the mantel and laid the long rifle on them. I knew then he wouldn't get shed of the rifle because Miss Susie liked squirrel meat best of all.

Along about the middle of the afternoon we saw two wagons going toward the river and when they got there

men, women and children piled out and began unloading
trunks, carpetbags and other truck. After the wagons were
unloaded, they turned back toward Humility. Men began
building a fire for the women to cook on. Then I saw Pleasant Tuesday Babson and I knew it was his party of pilgrims
he was taking to Texas. He must have seen Big Eli and me
for after a spell he came up the path from the river.

"Good house," he said, looking it over. "When do you
move in?"

"The wedding's tomorrow," Big Eli said. "We move in
right after."

"Sorry to miss it," Pleasant Tuesday said, "but the steamboat'll be coming by daybreak."

"I'd admire to have you," Big Eli said. "I took a hankering
to you."

"I reckon I did to you too, Wakefield," he said. "I had
hoped you'd join up with me. I'll be in need of a good hunter,
once we leave Louisiana."

Big Eli didn't say anything.

Pleasant Tuesday looked at me. "You're going to be a big
man when you grow up, Son," he said. "You'll need space to
breathe in. Come to Texas when your daddy weans you."

I grinned at him.

"Meantime, don't sleep in the same bed with grizzly bears,"
he said, smiling at me, and I knew he was thinking of the
night I ran away to Hannah.

"I won't," I said.

He shook hands with us and turned back down the path
to the landing.

Big Eli and I went back to work, picking up the log scal-
ings and sawed ends of timber which we took into the house
and stacked by the fireplace. It was getting close to sundown and I was wondering when we would knock off and
go back to Uncle Zack's. Big Eli took the rifle off the pegs.

"We'll eat here tonight," he said. "You feed the mule and
I'll go for squirrels."

He disappeared in the woods and in a few minutes I heard
two shots. Two others followed in a spell and soon he came

in with four squirrels. While he skinned and cleaned them I got a fire started in the fireplace. We roasted the squirrels on a spit stick and washed them down with spring water while outside it got dark and the folks at the landing started singing around their campfire.

After we ate, Big Eli sat staring into the fire but said nothing and I knew he was thinking of something he wanted to say but wasn't ready to say it.

"Will we sleep here tonight?" I asked him.

He shook his head. "No, we'll go back in a spell," he said.

I was standing with my back to the fire. He shoved a peg-leg stool my way and said, "Sit down, Little Eli. I want to talk to you."

I sat down.

"Little Eli," he started off like it was hard for him to find the right words, "you and I have been going where we pleased and doing what we pleased all of your life. We've had a good time and we never accounted to anybody for what we did or where we went."

"Until we came to The Purchase," I said.

He cleared his throat. "Tomorrow, I'm taking myself a wife and you're getting a mother," he said. "From now on we have to take her into account. We've got to do some of the things she wants us to do, though we may not like to do it."

"Like selling Faro," I said.

He nodded his head. "Yes," he said. "Miss Susie don't hanker hunting men. I had to sell him. And now I've got to get shed of something else. I can't do it myself, so I want you to help me out."

He got up from the hearth and reached for the Gabriel Horn. For a few seconds he stood there with it in his hands while the light from the fire played color on it. Big Eli loved the Gabriel Horn.

He handed it to me. "Take it in the hills somewhere so I won't ever find it," he said. "Dig a hole and bury it so nobody else will ever find it. And when you do that, Little Eli, make a vow never to tell anybody where you buried it."

I was too choked up to answer and I guess he was too for he hurried around and got a spade and lit the lantern. I slipped the thong of the Gabriel Horn over my shoulder, took the spade and the lantern, and stepped out into the dark. But the moon was just coming up over the distant ridges and I headed for them.

I didn't hurry for I had plenty on my mind, things I didn't understand. Big Eli mostly. I remembered the time, before we came to Uncle Zack's, when a she catamount caught Faro sniffing her cubs in a limestone cave and jumped him like a gust from hell. He didn't have a chance with that big cat and Big Eli was afraid to shoot for fear of killing Faro. Big Eli waded into the fight bare handed and got hold of the catamount's hind leg, then slammed the life out of her against the wall of the cave. He saved Faro's life, and for nearly two months we toted half our game kill to the mouth of the cave every night to feed the cubs until they were big enough to rustle for themselves.

Big Eli wasn't afraid of catamounts.

I had seen him fight a dozen men at Cadiz. I saw him whip the gamblers on the steamboat and I saw him beat Stan Bodine, a big man, within an inch of eternity.

Big Eli wasn't afraid of men.

And yet, Uncle Zack, a puny man, had whipped him. Mostly he had done it with money. Big Eli couldn't fight with money.

The coach driver on the Cadiz toll road had whipped him. Zybee Fletcher, the snake doctor, had whipped him. They had outsmarted him. Big Eli trusted people. He couldn't fight their way.

Miss Susie Spann had whipped him worst of all. She hadn't cut his hair, like I dreamed she did, and she didn't put a ring in his nose, but she had whipped him just the same. She had whipped him into the kind of man she wanted him to be and that wasn't the kind of man God made Big Eli to be. And when she whipped Big Eli she had whipped Hannah Bolen too, and I wondered if that was why, after all, she had whipped Big Eli and changed him so that Hannah wouldn't have him.

A steamboat moaned up the river before I got to the ridge I had in mind. Big Eli and I had spread the bear hide there on many a night and listened to Faro bay up and down the draws and more than once we had slept the night there under the stars. I knew Big Eli wouldn't be coming there again.

I put down the lantern and laid the Gabriel Horn next to it, then I slid the point of the spade under the top sod and lifted it easy so not to break it up too much. When I had enough sod laid aside, I dug a deep hole, then I picked up the Gabriel Horn but I didn't put it in the hole. I looked at it in the light of the lantern and the moon and I let my fingers slide along it like Big Eli had done before he handed it to me. It was smooth and curved like Hannah's arms.

Then it came to me that I had never blown the Gabriel Horn. I remembered what Big Eli had said, a long, long time before, when I asked him if I could blow it.

"It takes a man's wind to blow the Gabriel Horn," he had said. "Someday you'll grow up to it."

I had never asked him again. But as I stood there on the high ridge with the horn in my hands I began to wonder if I had grown up to it and had a man's wind.

I slid my wet tongue along my lips and drew them tight across my teeth like I had seen Big Eli do and then I raised the black tip of the Gabriel Horn to them. I sucked the chilly night air into my chest and let it fill my cheeks until they stuck out like a squirrel toting hickory nuts. When I could hold no more I pushed slow but with all my might and the air was filled with the music of it, sweet as a woman's song.

I felt the thin walls of the Gabriel Horn tremble as the pitch, high and sharp at first, trailed off deep into its own echo coming back from the far ridges. When they died away I was shaking all over, just knowing I had blown the Gabriel Horn and that I had a man's wind.

I had never felt that way before and I got warm all over and yet the sweat that ran down my neck was cold. For a second I wanted to blow it again, but I was afraid of that second blow and didn't do it. To myself and to Big Eli, if he heard it, I had proved I had a man's wind and the thought came to me that if I had a man's wind I was a man, and if I was a man I didn't need a mother even if Big Eli needed a wife. I thought of Hannah and I saw myself going into the tavern on the Paris road where Big Eli and I had seen her at last. I saw myself walking in with clenched fists and beating those men like Big Eli had beat the gamblers on the steamboat. I saw myself yanking a tooth out of the mouth of the tavern keeper, and taking Hannah in my arms and stalking out of the tavern to Uncle Zack's rig and taking her away from there.

Lights flickered on the surface of the river far below me and in the soft glow of the moon I could make out the steamboat. It broke the spell.

I knew I couldn't do the things I had just seen in my mind's eye. I wasn't a man. I was still a boy, just turned ten. I sat down by the lantern and buried my face in my arms and cried. I don't know how long I sat there for my heart was throbbing and there was thunder in my ears. I kept thinking about being a boy and not a man, and about Miss Susie's being my mother and I didn't want her to be.

It was then I heard something threshing through the hazel thickets below me and I remembered that Big Eli and I had seen the tracks of a Cinnamon bear near there only a month before. He had told me that a Cinnamon bear wouldn't attack a man, but I wasn't a man. I was a boy, and I was scared. I put out the lantern and edged into a thicket, then on my hands and knees I crawled as far as I could. I stopped to listen. I heard it ripping through the short brush where I had dug the hole to bury the Gabriel Horn and my heart slowed down a little. But soon it turned back and I knew it was following my trail. I still held the Gabriel Horn in my hand and I gripped the small end to use it as a club, but I was so pinned in I couldn't have swung it hard enough to hurt anything.

I felt a hot breath on my face and a long wet tongue began lapping my face like he was slobbering me up to make me easier to swallow. I was so scared I couldn't yell, but I put up my hand to shove it away. Then I felt the long floppy ears and I felt foolish and happy, wild happy. It was Faro and around his neck was a twist of rope. Somewhere, far off, he had heard the Gabriel Horn and come to me. I put my arms around his neck and buried my face against him while he whined and kept licking my hands. I began to crawl out of the hazel thicket, holding tight to the scruff of his neck because I knew I was never going to let him go again. But when we got out of the thicket, I remembered Miss Susie and Big Eli's promise to her. She didn't like hunting men. I knew I couldn't take Faro back there.

In the distance I heard the ringing of bells and two sharp blasts from the steamboat's whistle. It was pushing in to the landing to carry Pleasant Tuesday Babson and his pilgrims to the promised land of Texas. I had run away before and Big Eli had found me. But he had Faro with him when he did it. He didn't have him now. The steamboat would be long gone before he missed me and I wondered if, in the hustle and bustle of the pilgrims' getting aboard, I could stow away. A boy might do it where a man couldn't, even if the boy had a dog. We left the lantern and the spade beside the empty grave I had dug for the Gabriel Horn and headed for the river.

CHAPTER XXXIV

As I NEARED the landing, flames and smoke were pouring out of the stack of the steamboat and the wind, catching the sparks, dropped them into the river where they spit and sizzled. I doubled my pace for I knew the roustabouts were firing up to shove off. I glanced toward our cabin and saw no light. Big Eli, I was certain, had gone to look for me. The pilgrims were on deck and so was their plunder. The black roustabouts were still toting wood aboard. I held tight to the rope around Faro's neck and we kept to the underbrush, outside the rim of light cast by the fire from the open pits of the boilers. A black man, as big as Big Eli and stripped to the waist, was shoving cuts of wood into the pits where they glowed like tinder. The pilgrims were standing in a group on deck and I heard loud voices, but at the time I paid no heed to what was said, because I wanted to get aboard without being seen by Pleasant Tuesday Babson. He would have put us ashore.

I saw a roustabout, staggering under his load of wood, sway up the landing plank which sagged under the weight. Faro and I made a dash and went aboard behind him and if anybody saw us they must have thought we belonged to a pilgrim family. We skirted the boiler and hid between two rows of stacked firewood where we couldn't be seen. We had just settled down when the loud voices of the pilgrims came through the sizzling steam and they seemed het up about something. Still holding to Faro, I moved down the rows of firewood to listen.

"There's young'uns in this party, Mr. Babson, innocent little young'uns," I heard a woman say, and I reckoned she was talking to Pleasant Tuesday.

"She ain't a fitten' person to be amongst 'em," another woman shouted.

"She's an evil woman and she's not going, Babson," a man said, and another man backed him with cuss words.

"You put her ashore or we will," I heard a man with a high voice say and the crowd seemed to agree with him.

I looked around the row of firewood. The glare of the fire pits showed me everything there was to see, only I could hardly believe it. Standing back from the crowd and facing it was Pleasant Tuesday and beside him was Hannah Bolen. He had the fingers of both hands shoved under the bright yellow sash about his waist where the firelight glittered on the pearl and silver stocks of his fancy pistols. Hannah's arms were folded over her chest and there was a sort of smile on her face as she looked at the pilgrims crowded about the deck. I knew it was her the pilgrims had been talking about. But she wasn't scared like that time Doc Haney asked her questions after Stan Bodine was killed, or like the first night we got to Uncle Zack's and the Constable and Old Decker, the innkeeper from Cadiz, came to get her. It seemed to me, as I watched her looking at the pilgrims, that she was daring them to try and put her off.

"What're you going to do about her, Babson?" a man with his wife and two little girls beside him shouted at Pleasant Tuesday.

"I'll abide by her decide," Pleasant Tuesday said and looked at Hannah for her answer.

"God knows I've went by the best light I had," Hannah said, "and I'm staying aboard."

A skinny woman in a black bonnet spit at her.

Pleasant Tuesday didn't say a word. He swung around and called to two roustabouts.

"Pull in the plank," he said, and they dragged it on deck.

The captain must have been watching from the upper deck, for bells began clanging and the whistle shook the night air. I felt the boat shudder as the paddle wheel began to turn and churn the river into muddy foam. The big black roustabout was feeding wood into the fire pits with all his might and sweat rolled off his face and shoulders, making his hide shine like a polished boot leg.

When I looked again, Pleasant Tuesday and Hannah were still standing side by side facing the pilgrims. His hands were still close to the fancy pistols. Women were looking at their menfolks like they expected them to do something and men were looking at men like they were pondering which one would do it. I don't know for certain if it was the fancy pistols tucked under the yellow sash, or Pleasant Tuesday himself they were afraid of, but nobody did anything. It may have been seconds but it seemed longer to me that they stood staring at each other, the pilgrims and Pleasant Tuesday and Hannah. I wondered who would move first.

I heard the captain swearing and two more blacks began throwing wood into the pits and the big roustabout I had been watching stepped back to catch his wind and wipe sweat from his eyes. Then I saw that the boat hadn't moved from the landing and I remembered that Big Eli had warned Uncle Zack that the water was too shallow and the bed of the river too sloping for a good landing.

"A loaded boat'll founder at low stage," he had told Uncle Zack, but Uncle Zack had gone ahead with making it a landing anyway.

Now it had happened. The boat was stuck in the mud. I thought of Big Eli and wondered if we'd be free before he would come to the landing looking for Faro and me. I wasn't afraid of what he would do to me for he had never punished me, but I was afraid that he would blame Hannah and maybe Pleasant Tuesday too. I forgot about the crowd of angry pilgrims, and turned my eyes along the riverbank, which was bright as day from the fire and sparks pouring out of the stack, to watch for Big Eli. I wondered what I would do if I saw him coming to the landing before the boat got off the mud bottom. I wondered where I could hide that he wouldn't find me and Faro. Then I remembered the ice house on the steamboat we rode from Pekin. I didn't know whether this boat had an ice house or not, but I decided to go look for it. I knew it would be cold and dark but I figgered nobody would be looking in there until the cooks started fixing breakfast for the pilgrims. Big Eli, I was certain, wouldn't think to look for us in an ice house.

I had just made up my mind what I was going to do when there came a crash that seemed to split my ears and something whined over my head like a hant. I was knocked flat on the deck between the racks of wood and before I could get to my feet steam was whistling out of the boiler in a great white cloud that shut out everything but the red glare of the fire pits. I heard the pilgrims, men, women and children, screaming and carrying on.

I heard a man yelling "Lordy, oh Lordy, Lordy!"

The wind shifted the cloud of steam and I saw the big black roustabout with the shiny hide clawing at his eyes and twisting in pain, but his hide wasn't black and shiny like a boot leg but was white and puffed up like blisters on a yeast biscuit.

"Lordy, oh Lordy!" he kept wailing and then I saw him run to the downriver rail of the deck and topple over it into the river. For a few seconds he kept on wailing and yelling and splashing around and then was quiet and I never saw him again.

I looked around for Faro but he was gone. I hadn't heard him yelp and reckoned he wasn't hurt but just had the hair scared off him.

"Ca'm down, ca'm down!" the captain was screaming at the pilgrims from the second deck. "We only blew a valve is all!" I wondered if he had seen the black pit stoker go crazy and jump in the river.

I remembered Hannah and groped through the steam toward where she had been standing with Pleasant Tuesday. A shift in the wind lifted the steam from the deck again and I saw her. She was on her knees and at first I thought she had been hurt, but then I saw she was bending over somebody. It was Pleasant Tuesday and he had a deep gash in his head and I couldn't see his face for the blood. A piece of metal as big as my hand lay beside him and I reckoned that's what had hit him. Hannah glanced around when I stepped beside her.

"Where's Big Eli?" she asked.

"I don't know," I said, being too scared to say anything else.

She looked at the Gabriel Horn which was slung over my shoulder, then at me again. "What're you doing here?" she asked me.

"I'm going to Texas," I said.

For a second or so she didn't say anything but just looked at me. "We're both a far piece from being there now, Little Eli," she said and turned back to Pleasant Tuesday.

The pilgrims were crowding about us and women and young'uns were weeping and putting up an awful ruckus. The skinny woman in the black bonnet who had spit at Hannah fainted when she saw Pleasant Tuesday. Somebody threw a pail of water over her and others dragged her out of the way. The paddle wheel stopped churning the river and the captain came down and looked at Pleasant Tuesday. He dropped to his knees beside Hannah and slid his hand under Pleasant Tuesday's shirt.

Hannah said, "He's dead."

The captain nodded his head and got to his feet. "We'll bury him come sunup," he said, and called to the roustabouts to get spades and go ashore to dig the grave.

Hannah folded Pleasant Tuesday's hands across his chest and put his hat over his bloody face. A girl of about fourteen was having a convulsion and her eyes were bulging out like a bullfrog's while her folks held her down on the deck and tried to put a spoon between her teeth to keep her from biting off her tongue. Hannah went to them. The woman looked up and saw her and said, "It's a fit. She's had 'em before."

"Let go of her," Hannah said, and I knew she was vexed.

The man and his wife looked at Hannah and obeyed. The girl got to her feet and Hannah took her in her arms and they clunged to each other, the girl sobbing and Hannah talking to her soft and low.

I went to look for Faro, but I couldn't find him on the boat. The grave diggers had laid the landing plank so I went ashore and called him. I thought of blowing the Gabriel Horn to bring him back but I knew that might bring Big Eli too and I didn't want that to happen. Back from the river a hundred yards or more a lantern glowed in the dark and I heard spades striking the earth and the soft grunts of the roustabouts as they hefted the sod. I thought about Pleasant Tuesday and how he had come all the way from Texas to be buried without a box around him in a hole on the banks of the Tennessee. I liked Pleasant Tuesday and, in my mind, it wasn't a fittin' way to put him under. Of a sudden I didn't want to go to Texas without him and I didn't want Hannah to go either. I wanted to go back to Big Eli and I wanted her to go too, but I knew we couldn't. There was no place to go and I felt tired and heart-heavy.

It was too much for me to figger out. I wanted to be close to Hannah and talk to her and have her talk to me. I forgot about Faro and turned back to the boat. The pilgrims were still huddled together and making talk that sounded like argument. I pushed through them to Hannah who was listening to what was being said.

In the midst of them was Pleasant Tuesday, dead and growing cold, but they paid him no more heed than they had paid to the pit stoker who went crazy with pain and jumped overboard. I felt sorry for both of them. If I had been killed, I pondered, would I have been forgot so quick? I guessed I would, for I was no more than Pleasant Tuesday or the black spit stoker.

I heard one of the men say, "Texas is Spanish country and nary one of us has been there."

"Without him, they'll run us out," said another, and I knew they were speaking of Pleasant Tuesday and maybe they were feeling the same as I felt and didn't want to go to Texas without him.

"I'm for unloading our plunder here and now," said a woman, and most of the other women agreed with her.

"Make up your minds," the captain said. "When we've buried Babson and fixed the valve, I'm shovin' into the stream if I have to push us off the mudbank myself."

The pilgrims looked from one to the other, hoping somebody amongst them would make up their minds for them. Their faces looked as tired and weary as I felt and I saw some of the women crying, like they didn't want to go back and yet they had no place to go either. I wanted to ask Hannah what she was going to do, but before I had the chance I felt a warm hand brush my shoulder and rest light on it and somebody pushed between Hannah and me. I looked up to see who it was. It was Big Eli and Faro was at his heels. My knees began to shake, not from fear but because of a sudden I felt as light as a dove feather and I knew I must have been totin' a heavy load and the sight of Big Eli had lifted it off my heart.

His long fingers pressed into my flesh like they had found something they never wanted to let go of again and tears came in my eyes, but not from pain. Big Eli looked down at Pleasant Tuesday, studied him for a spell, and his right hand reached up for the keelboater's beaver which he tucked under his arm. He must have heard enough of the pilgrims' palaver to know what the trouble was, but the sight of Hannah and me pondered him and then a strange smile crossed his face when he saw the Gabriel Horn swinging from my shoulder. I knew then that he knew I had run away and why I had. He looked at the pilgrims who were still wrangling about getting off the boat.

"If you're a'mind to listen," he said to them, "I'd admire to speak."

The pilgrims turned toward him and quieted down.

"I'm going to Texas," he said.

A man in the crowd said, "Wakefield, you ain't never been to Texas."

Big Eli nodded. "I ain't never been to Heaven," he said, "but I hope to fetch up there."

"Amen," said an old woman. "I reckon we all do."

The pilgrims nodded their heads.

A woman stepped forward and looked at Big Eli with a sly grin. "Wakefield," she said, "I thought this was your weddin' day?"

Big Eli slipped his right arm around Hannah Bolen and drew her to him tight and firm. "I'm aimin' for it to be my weddin' day, mam," he said, "if I can find a preacher or a squire when the boat lands downriver at Pekin."